DAYS OF ALLISON

DAYS OF ALLISON

Eric Shapiro

A Crowswing Book

First published in 2006 by Crowswing Books.
PO BOX 301 King's Lynn Norfolk PE 33 OXW England
10 9 8 7 6 5 4 3 2 1
www.crowswingbooks.co.uk
First Edition
Text Copyright © Eric Shapiro 2006
Cover Illustrations Copyright © Ian Jarvis 2006
Introduction Copyright © Kealan Patrick Burke 2006

The moral rights of the author and illustrator have been asserted.
All rights reserved. No part of this publication may be reproduced, stored in a retrieval system, or transmitted, in any form or by any means, electronic, mechanical, photocopying, recording or otherwise without the prior permission of Crowswing Books.
All characters in this book are fictitious, and any resemblance
to real persons, living or dead, is coincidental.

ISBN 1-905100-20-5 trade p-b

Praise for Eric Shapiro

"Eric Shapiro's It's Only Temporary is an apocalyptic masterpiece: harrowing, hilarious, disturbing, heartfelt, and suspenseful. Not to be missed!" –James Rollins, best-selling author of Sandstorm and Map of Bones

"It's Only Temporary reads like a road movie travelling toward Armageddon, and its powerful, stylish writing and raw emotion will stay with you for a long, long time." Tim Lebbon, Bram Stoker Award-winning author of Desolation

"Relentless. Shapiro delivers a compelling narrative." –Jack McDevitt, Darrell Award-winning author of Eternity Road

"Eric Shapiro has created a gloriously horrific, touchingly intimate tale of the surreal reality of a world turned inside out; of one man's very human, very brutal struggle to 'grow the fuck up' as everything around him races headlong into madness." –Elizabeth Massie, Bram Stoker Award-winning author of Sineater

"Shapiro has crafted a damn near perfect Apocalypse story in It's Only Temporary; it shuns the usual trappings of the genre, concentrating on people and life rather than impossible schemes and crazy gadgets. A very engaging read!" –Michael Oliveri, Bram Stoker Award winning author of Deadliest of the Species

"Eric Shapiro has produced a manic road-trip story set at the edge of both the end of the world and his narrator's sanity. In spite of the energetic, farcical feel of the book, It's Only Temporary delineates eerily the all too credible behaviour that could occur in extreme circumstances." –Neil Ayres, author of Nicolo's Gifts

"This is a strange book for sure, but - if you're feeling strange - you'll find It's Only Temporary gripping and worthwhile. The apocalyptic tension builds to a climax that's equally surreal and realistic, while the characters' reactions in the face of death are chillingly believable." –Marty Beckerman, author of Generation S.L.U.T.

"A sweet tale wrapped in acid. Virtuoso storytelling, a wonderful blend of optimism and nihilism. Fierce and addictive, It's Only Temporary will stay with you a long, long time." –Adam Connell, author of Counterfeit Kings

"With a meteorite mere hours away from destroying humanity, Shapiro takes us on a riveting journey - a poignant coming of age story for a young man deprived of his future. Shapiro's writing is smart, funny, and refreshingly honest. It's Only Temporary is both a page-turning adventure and a thoughtful meditation on our existence." –Peter Buchman, screenwriter of Eragon and Jurassic Park 3

"I read It's Only Temporary in one fast sitting - it's the kind of slangy, stinging, pedal-to-the-metal stuff nobody does anymore - [Shapiro] could revive the entire Impending Doom genre - cool!" –Christopher Fowler, author of Full Dark House, and three time British Fantasy Awards winner

"I look for great things from Eric Shapiro..." – Kenoma Journal

"Shapiro has a knack for building tension..." –The Horror Channel

"...very reminiscent of the writing style of Harlan Ellison." – BookPleasures.com

Other Titles by Eric Shapiro

Short of a Picnic
It's Only Temporary
Strawberry Man

For Rhoda.

Introduction

So far this year, I've been asked to write eight introductions for various small press books, and I've turned down most of them, not because I have suddenly developed an ego or a sense of self-importance that gives me the power and inclination to disappoint those who, like me, are still swimming upward in the current-addled pool that is small press publishing, but because (a) I either didn't have the time when I was approached (hell, even this intro was about two months overdue), or (b) I wasn't a fan of the writer's work, and finding a couple of hundred, or worse, thousand, words of praise would have been too much of a chore, not to mention misleading to those eight or nine people who believe my opinion has some merit to it. Whatever the reason, telling a writer you can't pen the introduction to their book, knowing how hard they labored over it, is not a pleasant task or one I particularly relish, so whenever I'm sent something to read with a view to writing some kind words for it, I find myself hoping against hope that it's going to be good.

Eric Shapiro's "Days of Allison" is not good. It's outstanding. It also presents me with something of a predicament: How to talk about a story that really should not be talked about until you, good reader, have had a chance to read it. In that respect, I suppose an afterword would be more appropriate, but the tag on my shirt says I'm here to introduce, so introduce I shall.

"Days of Allison" is an intelligently and beautifully written science fiction tale, though categorizing it by one genre is a little unfair. There's a little bit of everything here–romance, horror, and humor, though not one bit of it comes across as being there for the sake of it, rather we are merely seeing life through the curious kaleidoscope of Louis's--our narrator's--eyes. It is his thoughts that amuse, and occasionally disturb, as we get to know his worldview intimately. It is the things he sees and his interpretation of them that we trust, no matter how peculiar they at times may seem. Shapiro wants the reader to trust Louis implicitly, to sympathize with his struggle, and this is achieved with an ease that will make many a writer envious of Shapiro's control over his world and the words he uses to weave it. We do sympathize, and empathize with Louis's plight because he's an average Joe, in some ways almost a subaverage Joe, the kind of guy we know or have seen and dismissed on our self-involved journeys elsewhere. Perhaps he's the kind of person all of us have been at some stage of our lives, or may yet become (a frightening thought in itself). He's no chiseled Adonis (quite the opposite, in fact); he's getting older, has little hair, works in an unsatisfying job, and is desperately lonely. Thankfully for poor old Louis–and herein lies the crux of Shapiro's excellent novella–he exists in a time where the dating game, courtship, and single bars have fallen into obscurity, and the technology is extant whereby ideal partners can be purchased already programmed as per your specifications. It's simply a case of selecting the look and the personality, even their spiritual beliefs, and your mate is delivered to your door, ready to go.

Obviously, for Louis, things don't go quite according to plan.

If you're thinking the idea sounds familiar, you'd be right. The concept of robots as mates is hardly a new one. Many of the science fiction genre's greatest proponents have delved into this psychologically intriguing notion at one time or another. Richard Matheson, Ray Bradbury, Isaac Asimov, and perhaps, most recently, and most often, Phillip K. Dick, liked to play with the idea that in the future, the cure to loneliness (and much, much more) will simply be a case of filling out some forms. Invariably, we come away with such moral fables with a not entirely positive message, as we watch the contentment of our protagonists start to falter when they realize that though made of synthetic skin and circuit boards, eventually machines will learn to think for themselves. And when they do, it is posited, they will yearn to be more like us, to envy us of only one thing: our soul.

But what is it that makes a soul? And for that matter, what is it that makes us human, makes us different from machines? Take away the materials in our composition, and what specifically is it that differentiates us from robots? Does consciousness beget a soul by default, or is it something more complicated, more spiritual than that? These are the questions that Shapiro tackles here, and though his basic concept is a well-worn one, his execution and delivery most certainly are not.

In "Days of Allison", when Shapiro introduces us to our lonely, conservative narrator, Louis has long resisted the fashionable trend of acquiring artificial mates. When we meet him, however, his resolve is starting to crumble. He senses that time is running out. He's ageing rapidly, with no prospects ahead of him, nor a wife at home to alleviate his ever-worsening sense of isolation and depression. Still he resists. In the end, it is his mother that intervenes to change his life. It's at this point in the proceedings that the imagination of the reader is truly ignited. You don't have to be lonely, or single, to wonder what it would be like to have the companionship of a mate designed entirely by you. Think of the possibilities! Being able to dictate how they look, specify their attributes from a blueprint you've only seen in dreams, and as for personality...pffft!...they'd be perfect in every way. You'd never argue, and if somehow you did, you'd already know the keywords to ensure you emerged victorious every time. They'd never complain; there'd be no rules but your own. Paradise, yes?

Somehow, I doubt it. More likely, after years of exposure to it, you'd find yourself wishing for a retort, a barb, a glass thrown in your direction. Passivity would become as bad as apathy, and you'd grow to resent it.

How many times in the past have you ended up with the girl/guy of your dreams only to later discover there were certain elements present that you hadn't counted on, elements no one could know without sacrificing their time and investing enough emotion to find out? Elements that ultimately ruined the relationship? If then, your mate was a robotic one, programmed to the core with everything you want, it could only end in disaster, and the fault would fall squarely at your feet, because by nature we don't know what we want, and that uncertainty would be reflected in our creation.

This, in particular, is what fascinates me about Shapiro's novella, and the concept in general: How perfect a mate can an imperfect man design?

Shapiro studies this in great detail, letting us get to know the very credible intricacies and eccentricities of his character before flipping the coin over and allowing us to see what makes Allison what she is, or what she is not. It's a compelling tale, and one that does everything right, leaving you wondering who the real artificial life-form of the story is, and forcing us to question everything we take for granted about human nature. It's a story about love, hate, and identity.

Phillip K. Dick would have been proud of this tale, and you, dear reader, have my envy that you're about to experience it for the first time.

Kealan Patrick Burke
Delaware, Ohio
September, 2006

Allison and I were together for 14 days.

My mother is behind all this. You could say, rightfully, that my mother is behind everything that's happened to me, as is every person's mother behind what's happened to them, for it is She who's responsible for this life of mine. Whether or not its humbleness and routines are best blamed on her is another matter altogether, but the life itself: her doing entirely. The life itself, and the fact that I'm in traffic when I could be home watching television.

The traffic is a necessary obstacle en route to Mother's home. I don't call her "Mother," mind you. I never call her that. Unless, that is, I'm thinking about her, in which case she looms – she always looms – in my mind as Mother. To her face, I call her Mom. Behind her back, I call her nothing, for I have no friends or siblings with whom I can discuss her. But to you, and in my head, she is Mother, and I sense (dread) she always will be.

Mother, no matter the extent of my academic and professional achievements, always wants more out of me. Perhaps this is symptomatic of me being an only child – I long ago gave up analyzing the matter. The consistent, perpetual, undying fact of the matter is that no matter what I do, it's never good enough. I lost twenty pounds last year, after which she told me I looked too thin. I gained back ten and was promptly deemed overweight again. Lost five, got treated like a sick person. Gained three just in time for her to drop the topic altogether.

This is my whole life.

The weight thing is a minor example well suited for polite company. Many other examples abound, most of them only suited for discourse among scumbags and lowlifes. For Mother, whatever her status amid the green grass pastures of suburbia, is a woman of true darkness. I say this with regrettable yet staggering graveness. Her darkness is not mild or grayish, but thick and velvety, deep and quite probably endless, suited for all manner of demon and vampire.

ERIC SHAPIRO

For example, shortly after pubic hair began sprouting between my legs, my mother got it into to her head that women were to be a part of my life. Well, to be fair, at that time it was "girls" she was interested in – not women; I mustn't accuse her of aiming to set up an adolescent boy with elderly ladies. And when I say *she* was interested in these girls, I couldn't be more serious, for I personally had no interest in the opposite sex, and to this day I still feel very little. My mother, on the other hand, seemed delighted by the idea of girls, specifically the idea of girls within the realm of *my* existence. She felt then, and continues to feel now, that I was secretly interested in females yet unable to admit as much, but I bid to you, in this private exchange, that I'm much better suited to be left alone.

My work and my books, that's all I need. If society ever relieves its inhabitants of the need to make money, then I'll quite eagerly sign up to be a hermit, eating, sleeping, reading my life away. Some would call this a lonely life, but whatever labels one may use, it is my life, my nature, and I value it greatly. Mother, however, deems me lonely. She tends to say, "I won't live forever, you know. Then you'll need another woman in your life."

If only she knew how I sometimes ache for her departure.

Needless to say, I am only joking. No son wishes for his mother's death. I only sometimes wish – very passionately – that Mother would shut her goddamn mouth every once in a while. Stop moving those lips, yap, yap, yap, and give my eardrums a chance to unwind. Sometimes, yes, in a very fantastical sense, this ache for silence morphs into visions of me standing at my mother's burial with a soft grin on my face, but these are only visions, not to be taken seriously or reported to establishments of law.

Perhaps the reason I protest Mother so actively in my mind is because I lack the courage to protest her in three-dimensional reality. Via some elusive bag of magic tricks, she is ever able to get me to do exactly what she wants. It's quite sickening, really.

When I was thirteen, Mother got it into her fevered mind that I should invite Little Sally from next door to the school dance. I quite hated this idea, loudly told my mother so, but to no avail: The dance concluded with me urinating on Sally's black patent leather shoes. This occurred right on the dance floor; my nerves had gotten the better of me, and the urine trailed down the inside of my leg before somehow accomplishing an upward leap from the bottom of my pant ankle onto Sally's shoes. Sally of course screamed and called me "Pisser Louis," the latter half of which is my actual name, the former half of which stuck with me through high school. Mother stopped demanding

DAYS OF ALLISON

I go on dates during high school, the relief of which was almost worth the shattering nickname. She knew by then, with a constant sigh in her mouth, that her son was unpopular, and best suited for long nights alone on the sofa.

Before I knew it, the real world came, and that's when Mother resumed her little (in fact tremendous) fantasy. By then, "women" indeed became the applicable target of her ideals. I was to find a woman, love a woman, procreate, and exist in a state of echoing joy unto eternity. At least that's the way Mother pictured it; my mind only conjured more and more scenarios involving frightened piss.

She begged, Mother did. If her knees weren't bad, I'll bet she'd have got down on them. She said to me, "Please just branch out a little, Louis. Lonely people don't know how lonely they are until they make friends."

To which I once replied, "That's true. I'm at my loneliest around other people."

I believe she nearly choked on her supper at that remark. When she recovered, she took her usual approach toward persuasion: calling me awful names. "You're just a lousy idiot, aren't you, Louis?"

"More like a son of a bitch," I corrected her.

We didn't speak for months. I was in heaven.

Like with all our other tiffs, though, she eventually recovered, only to resume a rigorous schedule of making me insane. Our conversations were uniformly tense, laden with swears and half-whispered insults, until the day when she mentioned the notion of a robot.

I remember it fully; we were on the phone. A pause overcame me when she said the r-word. Every instinct in my central nervous system told me not to fall for it, that there had to be a catch, for this was, after all, Mother speaking. But in retrospect, those instincts were on autopilot, geared to reject anything the old woman said. Quite in fact, the idea appealed to me. I had seen the ads on television, but never once thought they could apply to my own life. (I don't tend to think beyond my daily regimen.) Suddenly, though, the concept took on full color, and I became energized, even somewhat aroused. Understand now, that these positive emotions were, like all my emotions, largely remote, yet I could not deny their tickle.

For a robot was different, no? Female, certainly, in every respect – so much so that the majority of people would be unable to detect her unnatural origins – but definitively safe and nonjudgmental. Unmarred by the countless stains of an authentic social existence; no oppressive sense of conformity, in other words. All my quirks and failings would be meaningless in the midst of her artificial consciousness. Her mental environment would be a blank plot of land upon which I could build anything I wanted to.

As with all things in my life, the progression was slow. Eighteen months have passed between Mother's first mention of robots and my present ride to Mother's house, to pick up Allison.

* * *

There are presently four major global companies that manufacture robots for domestic use, and two minor ones. I'm certainly not an expert, but I believe the first of the lot was Animedia, a company out of San Jose, California. Animedia was originally created as a distributor of pets. The company's founder, a mad-looking but apparently sharp-minded individual by the name of Neidlinger, perceived, rightfully, that given the short lifecycles of authentic domesticated animals, said animals' owners were too often the victims of despair. To eliminate the regular mourning cycles of the traditional pet enthusiast, Mr. Neidlinger (his first name eludes me, but newspapers can fill in the blanks on any given day) invented synthetic pets, the biological accuracy of which was nothing short of alarming. I for one was terrified by the development, but truth be told, I tend to be terrified by developments of every sort.

This new breed of animals, cleverly nicknamed "Animedials," was astounding in terms of the attention to detail they boasted. Less than one year after they hit the marketplace, I had an occasion to hold one in my lap. My cousin Sheila and her husband Len had invested in a poodle, and it was so lifelike, so limitlessly tactile and fully realized, that I had to stifle the pulsing urge to throw it – fast and hard – straight through Sheila's living room window. The perfection of its hair – not so smooth as to seem fake, but just matted and damaged enough to seem too real – was the first thing that struck me. Then came the rhythm of its "breath," not real breath, mind you, just a motorized pumping of the chest which will likely continue happening long after Len and Sheila (if not every other organism on Earth) are dead. One would expect, given the efficient nature of most machinery, that the poodle's breathing would go on at a regular, monotonous pace, but no – Mr. Neidlinger would dream of no such predictability. The poodle breathed faster when it ran, slower when it was asleep, sometimes through its nose, sometimes even – much to my resounding horror – let go a vicious sneeze. As if the hair and the breathing weren't enough, there was the dog's propensity for erections, long red ones, which its tiny internal chips and gears made sure occurred whenever it rubbed up against something soft – or nothing at all. Humping, of course, was an important part of this program. But it wasn't (though I shiver to admit this) the erections that nearly made my nervous system collapse. It was, finally and for certain, the little creature's eyes.

I use the word "creature" intentionally, for Bastard (that's what they named the poodle) is very much alive within the currents of my subconscious. And his eyes are the reason for this. They are neither dark nor shallow, like the buttons one sees on a doll's face, but shimmering and deep, leading to an inarguable consciousness. Whether that consciousness is rich or simplistic is open to infinite debate, but its utter existence is not. Bastard is *aware* of me, and Sheila, and Len, and Mother, and the postman, and everyone and everything, and for a long time I thought Animedia was nothing other than the devil's workshop.

Alas, the human brain, much like the cultures it inhabits, has a way of absorbing new things, even shocking ones. Before long, lest there be a monopoly on domestic robotics, RealPets was formed elsewhere in the Silicon Valley, then Fluent Dynamics, Inc., over on the East Coast, just outside of Washington, D.C. And later (though some unpatriotic souls like to theorize that they came first), Japan gave us The Playtime Group, or at least that's what they call it in the English translation. Each company brought its own creativity to the table. Animedia was of course the pioneer, so they glowed with a sheen of corporate integrity and wisdom, short on new innovations but long on confidence, not to mention a fervent commitment to their guiding principles: relaxation, longevity, authenticity, and plain old fun. For my money, their TV commercials boast the finest photography, always very sharp, and often with a touch of pink or purple to set the mind swooning. RealPets tried to trump Animedia by boasting that all of their products were one of a kind, and that their impersonation of God was therefore more divine than the one engaged in by the Neidlinger outfit. Fluent Dynamics bragged of superior motion technology, i.e., its cats and dogs ran faster and smoother, its birds' wings fluttered more naturally, its tigers' tongues licked their noses in a more biologically sensible manner. (I forgot to mention that, given the inauthentic nature of these animals, all kinds of creatures quickly became suited for domestic environments, providing the world with pacifistic lions and friendly wolverines. The gentleman living downstairs from me even owns an elephant; I'm just grateful he's not upstairs.) The Japanese brought my personal favorite innovation to light: Their animal products boast the most convincing fecal matter, complete with an offensive stench. Leave it to the Asians to squeeze in a good chuckle while changing the world.

    This song and dance went on for a good while, something like a decade, and meanwhile actual pets began to fall out of favor. Even the liberal activists eventually had to cede to the fact that an immortal furry friend was better than one who's capable of dying on you. With no shortage of irony, the vast majority of the actual pets in developed nations were punished for their mortality – via death itself! Many a traditional pet store closed down, sending all its stock to be eliminated (i.e., set on fire) somewhere on the outskirts of town. And meanwhile, not too far in the background, the public debate about animal rights shifted to a public debate on a far touchier subject: The invention and subsequent marketing of robotic humans.

    As one might expect, RealPets lead the way in this regard. What with their specialty of creating unique stock, they had a God-given advantage (pun very much intended). They formed a division called RealPeople, which, after a media uproar, was promptly renamed RealMates within seventy-two hours. Apparently, some actual real people were offended by the competition (I'll bet most of them had weight problems). Much to the chagrin of more than a few Congressman, the director of RealMates called a national press conference, at which he shared the following insights: "The human race has found inspiration in the immortality and complexity of the new life forms among which it finds itself" – cheers to him for avoiding any mention of "robots" – "and RealMates is intent upon advancing this life-affirming journey. Within the month, our first line of sensitive and compassionate Mates will be ready to make your acquaintance."

    One had to hand it to the guy: Not once did he stoop to words like "manufactured" or "crafted" or "designed." Not that it mattered, anyway: Most people were delighted by the notion no matter what semantics were in play. I was merely a boy at the time, and still a little nauseated by the whole business, but, as you well know by now, also quite credibly intrigued.

* * *

    Mother is lurking; she always lurks. Here I am, finally out of the God awful traffic, and can she even look me in the eye? Can she even pause for one moment, stop shuffling back and forth about the kitchen, and address me head-on, as though I'm some sort of *human being*? No, instead she lurks. She checks the cabinets, opens and closes the refrigerator. I haven't seen her eyes in several years. Bastard the poodle's eyes are more vivid in my mind than hers are.

DAYS OF ALLISON

"Where is she?" I ask, as my mother pumps a brown loaf of bread on the top shelf of the fridge.

"In the closet."

"In the closet?" I'm astounded. "I thought you couldn't turn them off."

"You can't," she says, turns the bread around, clockwise, counter-clockwise, twists the buttons on her sweater. Touches her hips, closes the fridge door, opens it an inch – a rubbery sigh from the door's lining – then closes it again.

I find myself nearly shouting, both from the news of Allison's location in the closet and from Mother's uncontrollable metabolism: "If you can't turn them off, then that means my girlfriend is now standing in the closet, unattended, in sheer darkness!"

"Shhh!" Mother hisses, spraying one pale finger with saliva. "She can hear you, probably!"

"Oh? And what's wrong with that? Does she not know she's in the closet?"

Mother finally stands still. Her hands are balls upon her hips. She stares right into my chest, her version of eye contact. "Of course she knows where she is. I just don't want her knowing her new companion has a temper."

I look straight into Mother's eyebrows (the only things visible, since her eyes themselves are aimed toward the yellow floor): "Perhaps you're forgetting the fact that I'm her *owner*. Her companion, yes, that too, but her owner, more importantly, and I doubt she'll object to any behavior whatsoever on my part."

"Who's paying the monthly installments?" Mother asks me.

"Who's living with what you're paying for?" I ask Mother.

Not too long after that exchange, I find myself standing before Mother's hall closet, some three feet away, my heart pounding against my chest, the doorknob glaring at me like a judgmental golden eye. I dare not touch it, for beyond this thin wooden sheet stands my future.

I whisper to Mother, who stands closer to the door: "What if I don't like her?"

Mother shrugs, her sweater brushing her earlobes. "She has all the traits you put on the order form. Beauty, personality, spunk."

"But she's also from RealMates," I argue. "They're all *unique*." That last word like poison, sizzling up my mouth.

"Something tells me you'll get along just fine," Mother assures me, but, like all her assurances, it sounds menacing, somehow layered, as if her heart isn't in it, or worse, she has no heart.

Mother's hand is on the doorknob. I go into a haze of adrenaline

so thick that before I can prevent it, the door is no longer there.
I am face-to-face with Allison.

For a long while, I had a distant, dysfunctional relationship with the word "beauty," as though it were a mysterious, superior stranger whom I had no right to deal with or address. Beauty was something other people spoke of, more worldly, sophisticated people, the likes of which I hardly knew or understood. And when they spoke, they spoke of streams and mountains, imperial things, and yes, of course women, always women: their cheeks, their eyes, their swelling breasts. But all the while, in the midst of such discussions, I lingered in the background, at the peripherals, for I had nothing whatsoever to add. Truth be shared, I rarely have anything to add to most conversations. More truth be shared, most of the conversations which I overhear occur within the realm of my TV screen, so my whole metaphor about being in the background is a falsehood: I'm really on my couch. Certainly, I speak to some people at the office, and my conversations with Mother tend to travel some distance some of the time, but what I'm trying to impart is: Throughout my life, when people – on television, on the street, aboard the subway, overheard at restaurants – spoke of beauty, I had nothing – outwardly *or* inwardly – to add.

Until I laid eyes upon Allison.

The sheer level of hokey sentiment in that statement is astounding, so very much clichéd, so pathetically devoid of a detectable shred of authentic life experience on my part. Nonetheless, it is the truth, and if not the absolute, God's-eye truth, then at least sincerity: I mean it. To linger over her respective physical features one by one would be a dreadful bore, not because said features are boring in-and-of-themselves, but because it's not the features themselves which hypnotize me, but their essence, their striking air of white-lit divinity. Something floats around Allison, and flows from her, and forgive my reverie, but she strikes me as wholly non-mechanical. Her eyes don't click when she blinks; her neck doesn't swish when she cranes it; her voice never creaks or crackles when she speaks. Whatever logical, cerebral awareness I have that she is not real has been overridden by a cloud of sweet emotion, running all the way from my tickled mind to my stirring legs.

It's the eye contact that gets to me most. Mother, as I've shared, is not a great fan of the activity. Whenever I do have an occasion to lock eyes with Mother, I tend to be left cold by the experience. There is something very much tangled within Her essence, something dank and worrisome and mildly apocalyptic. Despite her many friends and bridge partners, mother has never traded much in the commerce of charm. She deems it a trade best suited for weaklings and hopeless romantics. I cannot judge her for this, of course, because I myself am uniformly charm-less. Once was a time when I tried to make jokes or light remarks to those around me – this was during my first few days at my job – and they seemed offended by my advances, made silent, amused eye contact with one another, shared some secret that I dare not attempt to untangle.

Allison, on the other hand, unlike Mother and myself, has some sort of clean blue electricity behind her eyes, within them I should say, a sort of curiosity and hunger that pokes at some moist patch in the collective consciousness of all living creatures, the patch from which hope and excitement and soft kisses sprout. The phenomenon of Allison's eyes (and yes, I do see now that I've resorted to the too-tired practice of discussing her in bodily terms) is altogether inspiring and – cheer me on as I embrace the word – beautiful.

To watch her moving about my apartment is to watch a kind of perpetual ancient dance. Though I am constructed of blood and tissue, she has grace that I could never imagine emitting from my own person. She is a purified amalgam of everything sensual and womanly in the annals of recorded human history. In her presence, I am intensely reminded of pop love songs, great romantic movie scenes, and – no reason to suppress this – the gentler side of pornography. Some would argue that pornography has no gentler side, so to explain: I am referring to pornography with soft lighting, creamy-skinned actresses, and minimal outright genital coverage. Not soft-core, quite, but that careful realm on the line between hard and soft; tasteful enough to be pleasant, but shocking enough to keep viewers awake.

Mother spoke of beauty, personality, and spunk, but all told, I believe the sheet had slots enough for twelve different traits, three physical, three emotional, three psychological, and three spiritual. (Atheists are allowed to pass on the "spiritual" section in favor of a convenient "other" section.) If I recall correctly, my specifications were as follows:

DAYS OF ALLISON

Physical: beauty, red hair, blue eyes.
Emotional: strong personality, adventurous, spunky.
Psychological: resilient, sincere, searching.
Spiritual: agnostic (leaning toward belief), pacifistic, Buddhist.

I know very little about Buddhism, but I believe I'm correct in guessing that it has something to do with beauty, so the parallel dictated the choice. Then, farther down the sheet, a fascinating philosophical question struck me like a blow:

Would you like _____ (the blank was a line for my chosen robot name) to be aware of the fact that she/he ("she" comes first because most robots that sell are female) is not human?

This was quite possibly the hardest decision I've ever made. While Mother paced about her kitchen, I sat there quietly, holding my silver pen by the outermost particles of my fingertips, letting it sway. The implications and complexities were too vast to recount here, but allow me to touch upon the basics.

First off, most real people cannot tell a robot from one of their own. The technology has become so sophisticated that robots not only look authentic, but speak and behave with complete adherence to the patterns laid out by nature. I even recall a "Guess the Robot" game show that was promptly cancelled once its producers realized how few contestants were capable of winning. "You must be some kind of robot" jokes are painfully common fodder for sitcoms and stale commercials. Taking such things into account, it occurred to me how frustrating life must be for robots who know they are robots, how left out they must feel, being taken for humans but knowing, not even deep down inside, but right there on the surface, that they are fundamentally different, that they have no past and an infinite future.

Robots who are programmed with human identities occupy a much more functional column of the population. They have rich, colorful pasts and a deeply entrenched sense (albeit false) of their own mortality. They're also known to be much more engaged in the ebb and flow of society and culture: many of them seek out jobs and careers, or engage in volunteer work or artistic endeavors to quench their humane appetites. Most critical to this discussion is the fact that they age. In the early days of Animedia, this was unheard of, a far-off lunatic fantasy, but leave it to the Japanese scientists to unearth the key: When a robot's mind is programmed to believe in its own mortality, its body follows suit by growing, growing, developing, then declining, slowing down, growing "ill" (not truly ill, but symptomatically so) and ultimately deteriorating. To be sure, actual death does not result. The only thing that can irreversibly conclude a robot's earthly existence is a substance called toxocin, most of which is kept stowed away behind weighty steel doors in large, studious laboratories. When a human-thinking robot's aging process gives way to deterioration, its manufacturers are alerted by computer and show up at its home, usually in the thick of night, and inject a tiny dose of toxocin into its neck. Whatever follows is up to theologians to decide.

Needless to say, as I sat there filling out the form, I was leaning very heavily toward the robot-as-human dynamic, but one little thing, one overpowering little thing, gave me serious pause. A little word that I try to bow down to whenever I can: truth. Though a human-thinking robot would perhaps be more relatable – nothing, I imagine, beats staying up late into the night and trading old tales of childhood – it would ultimately be living a lie. And not only that, but I, as its keeper, would be the guardian of that lie. What would happen, I wonder, if one were to look a humanized robot in the eye and sneer, "You're not human, you silly fool"? God knows I personally would never be so cruel, but the question's deeper meaning is clear: A robot walking around believing he or she is human is dangerous.

Not in the physical sense, heavens no. By and by, robots never commit crimes of any sort, including misdemeanors. I'm referring to psychological danger. Spiritual danger. Existential. The load of an entire artificial identity may have buried repercussions of which we are presently unaware. Robotic technology has only thrived for the past two decades, so who can determine – in the long-run – if it's best to let some robots walk around living a lie? I'm no priest or psychologist, but the notion caused me concern. And besides, as a person, I am so prone to keeping my personality under wraps that I could see no good in having a Mate whose true identity was under thicker wraps, technological ones at that.

So I rolled the dice and told them to program Allison with the truth. Not only did the choice make me feel righteous, but it's also rather exotic: Kind of sexy (borderline bestial) to shack up with a mate from another "species." As a bonus, Allison will never age. When I die, she will be able to apply for a Free Motion certificate, allowing her to live life as she fancies.

About now, what she fancies is an evening of love. Just after midnight, as I stuff some bill envelopes on my living room coffee table, she saunters down the steps in a trim blue nightgown (a tiny but eclectic wardrobe came with the package). She looks at me, and doesn't speak. She *purrs*:

"What do you like to do for fun, Louis?"

My mind is a euphoric blank.

It occurs to me as my penis is deep within Allison's vagina that she is convincingly organic through and through. Part of me expected a crunch of plasticity up inside her, a bit of startling coolness, perhaps a pane of metal, but alas, we have flesh and moisture, oozing, the latter, more and more of it as we go harder and harder, and I marvel at not only the beauty of her breasts and the sparkle in her aqua eye (only one eye catches the light from the window), but the delights – oh! joyous! – of technology itself.

I must confess (though any intelligent and reasonable listener has deduced as much by now) that Allison is my first lover, and perhaps, in objective reality, her genitalia feels far different from that of an actual, earth-born lady, but instinct strongly tells me otherwise: Plainly stated, she feels the way pornography looks. Her texture, to my touch, is identical to the "dirty" images that have often met my eyes. To be sure, one could argue that pornography, like Allison, is not real, but that argument collapses when one considers that most pornography (unless otherwise labeled) involves mammals, not machinery, thereby validating pornography as a frame of reference for my claim that Allison feels like An Actual Woman.

(For the record, I personally have never seen, much less rented, a robot porn movie. I don't very much comprehend the point of doing so. Supposedly, the "actors" (though "puppets" is perhaps a more accurate word) in robot porn are programmed (or "willing," depending on how you feel about free will) to do crazier things: bestial, scatological, sadistic, masochistic, humiliating. Rumor has it that some underground companies have invented robotic children – namely schoolgirls – for distribution to kiddy pornographers, but I find that hard to believe given how ridiculously expensive artificial beings are to manufacture. If the rumors are true, I hope the kiddy bots are of the truth-aware variety, which would save them from the inevitable pain of aging.)

I have lapsed into a dissertation on X-rated movies when my

desired focal point is truly Allison, forever, always Allison. I suppose my lapse is inevitable given my embarrassing lack of sexual experience. Nonetheless, I must part with the programming of smut films and fully enter this new universe: a place of wide white plains and eternal, crystalline longing. Now that masturbation has exited my existence, my true love life shall consist of beauty and tenderness. Robot mate or not, I wouldn't dream of any other approach.

It then occurs to me – another inevitability – that I'm guilty of my own falseness here, for Allison, of course, has been programmed to bed me. The only reason she didn't do so on our first night together, upon our return from Mother's house, is that she was experiencing what the pundits term "Entrance Sickness" (ES), a variant of motion sickness experienced when an artificial life form orients him or herself in the natural world, testing out the senses, getting used to the body, et cetera. We must remember that Allison has just been born, so to speak. (A surge of guilt crackles through me: Am I in bed with an infant? Oh, shut up, Louis!) Robots are not prone to anxiety, but some dizziness and confusion is inevitable during any bout of ES. And I'm sure Mother's thoughtful decision to lock Allison in a closet didn't help matters. But let's not think about Mother while I'm screwing.

Another crackle, this one not guilty so much as creepy: *Allison has no mother.*

Will you please quiet yourself, Louis? Your erection is at stake here. No more existentialism. The only abyss you should be leering into is the one between Allison's thighs.

She was born from nowhere.

Shut up!

How can she exist?

Above me, seemingly twelve feet away, Allison pinches and twists her luscious pink nipples. As she does so, I reach up and stroke her knuckles with my open palms. She giggles, shows me her tongue. Such a warm smile on her face, empty of judgment, of anything but pleasure and respect.

Just like they programmed her to.

Sad, isn't it? They don't even ask you on the order form what kind of attitude you'd like your RealMate to have toward you. Subservient, unflinching respect is the norm, the mainstream. Whenever I'm out in public and I see a wife treating her husband awfully nice, or vice versa, I don't think, "Well, isn't that nice?" Instead I think, "Well, isn't that high-tech?"

I need to break loose from my head. Get out of my big head and into my little one, more specifically. How 'bout some dialogue? Talk

DAYS OF ALLISON

dirty. Engage your mate's mind.

"Do you love me?" I ask her, cupping those breasts.

No need for handicapping here. Call off all the bookies. There is a one hundred percent chance that Allison will say yes. It's required, locked in. If she doesn't say yes, she's defective. Yet, like an actor in a play, I await my co-star's answer with a deeply felt, though plainly artificial, sense of unpredictability.

She rides me, she rides me, she rides. That mouth, those eyes.

"Yes, I do, Louis. I'll always love you."

Always! Splendid.

Even in two hundred years? When I'm dead and you're still walking around?

Before I get sucked into the quicksand of that question, a shot goes through me. As I quake to a finish, Allison throws her head back, laughs and screams. Both blue eyes catching the light.

I had a cyst behind my knee as a child. Hard like rubber, imperfectly round; I hungered to see it, to know its color, be able to touch its underside, the part that was imbedded in my flesh. It was benign, of course, which is why I'm still here, but hard, I tell you, so irritatingly hard. How I desired to steal a pin from Mother's sewing kit and stick it through that cyst. Would that kill it?, I wondered on a daily basis. Would a blast of air hiss out?

Only later did I learn, after the doctors opened my knee and carved it away, that the thing was full of fluid, not air. Creamy, soupy fluid, yes, but fluid all the same, and I wondered how liquid of any kind, anywhere in the world, let alone inside my leg, could be so thick as to make the cyst throb as fully as it did. Its hardness seemed to run through-and-through, but alas, the doctors explained to me, it was only a surface thickness, intensified by the ongoing swell of pus.

"Can I see it?" I ask the doctors, masks on their faces, standing over me with glowing tools. "After you take it out of me, can I see what it looks like?"

Smiles behind their masks. I can't see the smiles, only their outlines. "Why of course you may, son," comes a voice, echoing, from behind one mask, I can't tell which.

Yet, when I wake up, the nurse tells me they have thrown the cyst away. I silently curse the doctors. My prize, my only consolation, thrown away idly, in the hopes that I'd forget.

Today, in my thirties, I still remember. Sometimes in the night, as the weeds of sleep flick up around my head, I think about that cyst lying in a junkyard somewhere, its glass vial cracked open, mosquitoes dipping their snouts into it, sucking out the juice, the thick juice, so thick it explodes their ribcages and snaps their backs, but they glory in it all the same, for its tender, bloody flavor and its organic human origin. Then the mosquitoes die happily with my thick pus swelling in their guts, little smiles on their microscopic faces.

What color was that cyst? In the hospital, I used a mirror to search the hole behind my knee, look for remnants of the tumor, a few remaining particles. Even at that young age, I knew my search was to be in vain, leaving me with only guesses in my mind: black cyst, brown cyst, red, yellow, tan, green. Swelling swelling swelling

like this nightclub Allison made me take her to. The weekend has almost vanished, and we must, she insists, turn away from our bodies for pleasure, and venture out into that place with which I have next to no authentic familiarity: the world.

As Allison breaks an artificial sweat (part water, part sea salt) out on the dance floor, a blonde across the way makes brief eye contact with me, nothing suggestive or provocative, just curious, if even that, and I look back and marvel at how completely turned off she'd be if she knew the man in the neatly pressed suit near the bar whom she just glanced at was thinking about cysts and junkyards and surgery and thirsty bugs. Does a woman like her ever have such thoughts? Such women seem to devote their existences to suppressing such matters, or at least pretending to suppress them. I once read somewhere that men are naturally inclined to be more cerebrally perverse than women; can't recall why. And I imagine that even if I were to sit this blonde down and explain to her that I'm thinking about my old cyst because the swell of its liquid reminds me of the swell of humanity (synthetic and otherwise) within this club, I imagine she'd roll her eyes and flex her ass rudely as she walked away.

Allison, however, of course – of course – wouldn't dare to judge the wanderings of my twisted mind. I wonder if eye-rolling is even enfolded within the limitless intricacies of her programming. Probably somewhere, but never when it comes to me. Look at her, looking at me. Such charm, so natural – and I don't mean natural to her, I mean natural to the world. Nature. I'm no more equipped than any person to prove the existence of a soul, but I reckon the first place to start looking for proof is on the surface of Allison's face. And if no proof is to be found, that is of no consequence whatsoever, because, in order to keep living with her and not fall into a black panic, I have to believe in her soul. Our union (like all unions, I imagine), requires a measure of faith in greater powers.

Look at her dancing! Her body a blast of pure animal electricity, such fluidity and spark, the sexiness of her hair as it swings to and fro, the holy slope of her lower breasts, the smile – the smile! – lighting up her face. My blood tap-dances through my veins, does a wild tap number on the surface of my brain. This is love; it has to be.

"Some hot piece of ass, that woman!" a bloke to the left screams into my temple, slicing through the techno beat, not to mention the tissue guarding my eardrum. He's looking at Allison, of course, and then at me, then at her, his eyes wild and stirring. I dare not turn fully toward him, but my peripheral vision reports to me that his head is bald – how else could it so perfectly reflect the blue-green lights swimming aimlessly overhead? – and his muscles steely and perfect. Perhaps he's not even human, but then again, per my recent switch to faith: Aren't we all human?

"Very nice indeed," I say back to the man, and wonder what the proper etiquette is in such an exchange. Do I share with him outright that Allison belongs to me (both in essence and on paper), or would that constitute a rudeness capable of damaging his apparently blissful reverie? One thing is for certain, though I'm slightly embarrassed to admit it: I do desire to continue chatting with this gent, for my brain has gone about producing images of he and I advancing to a permanent and respectful friendship; him having my back, me having his. I see us lunching together in my office cafeteria during the off hours, my coworkers looking on in amazement, muttering to one another, "Louis has a *friend*?"

But of course this fancy is entirely ludicrous, and all the more embarrassing therefore. My brain drifts off into such tangents every single time a stranger of any sort, in any location, says anything whatsoever to me. I can't help it; it's psychological leftovers from the days when Mother used to more actively encourage me to branch out and make friends. I wonder briefly if all lonely people put on such shows inside their heads, but my wondering is cut short upon a longer glance at Allison, who makes me realize, with a jolt, that I'm no longer all that lonely.

In any case, lest my pause go on too long, I continue my conversation with the bald man by saying, "She's my girlfriend." Rude or otherwise, it has the benefit of being entirely true, so if his feelings are hurt, I cannot be held accountable.

I now sense the man looking at me, "up and down" as the expression goes, and unless my peripheral vision is dealing out falsehoods, I sense something of a snarl about his mouth. A vague sense of concern is tickling me, so I go about flexing my head and looking his way, at which point I see for certain that he's not hurt – no, not at all – but shocked!

Although I was kind enough to think twice before venturing into perceivable rudeness, this man engages in no such introspection. He hisses at me, breath stinging my eyes: "Yeah, right! Some length that'll last! What you got, a loaded bank account?"

Fear is an emotion I'm familiar with, but not at this level of intensity.

DAYS OF ALLISON

Suddenly my intestines are knotted; my blood stops dancing in my head and starts jogging through my calves. I then go about the business of formulating a witty, snappy, timeless, and memorable comeback, the likes of which will sting my new "friend" so hard that in all likelihood he will adjourn to the bar and drink himself into a violent death. My brain makes speedy, nimble calculations, considering his words, their tone, his meaning, his breath, rapidly scanning the rolodex for something swift and cutting, but before I'm even close to parting my dry lips, the man has gone.

Little did he know that it's not me, but Mother, with the bank account, and that although Allison is indeed with me because of money, she had no conscious choice in the matter. And there I go thinking all existentially again, about choice and will and freedom and truth, and before I know it my fear has taken a right turn down an alley dark with anger, and I'm on the dance floor stomping toward Allison, intent upon dragging her home before anybody else takes it upon themselves to judge our intimate relationship.

"Come home with me, love," I growl at her, gripping her by the elbow, the sweat of which is so convincing that I won't ponder it until later, when I'm washing my hands before bedtime.

And this, dear friends, is when things take a turn, the moment at which all my idle, quiet anxieties about Allison and the Meaning of it All morph into outright obsessions, the juncture from which there is no returning, for Allison looks at me, a sharpness in her eyes, not altogether kindly, and snaps her arm away, the slipperiness of her sweat proving helpful to the motion. And she says to me, in that human voice, as other beings and entities dance wildly around us: "Don't call me 'love.' I don't love you."

And so our story authentically begins.

Frannie has an affection for cigarettes. To be honest, I'm surprised she's been alive for as long as she has, given the way she eats and smokes. Late sixties (maybe early seventies, considering her penchant for lying), whitish hair, yet she still has energy to burn. Perhaps all the junk she puts into her body is somehow propelling it. I've never in my life seen an obese senior citizen, for death usually claims them before senior citizenship can. Frannie sets a new, astounding record.

    I wait for her to step outside for a smoke. This takes forever. Usually, on most days, she'll do anything, conjure up any excuse you could think of, to stand up from her desk, straighten the wrinkles from her burgundy skirt, and loudly croak, "Well, I could use a break, by God." Then she'll return twenty or so (sometimes thirty, once forty-five) minutes later wreaking of tobacco and flowing with a cheap, brownish calmness. All those minutes aren't spent smoking, I can assure you that. There's a newsstand across the street from our building, complete with a creaking rack of old romance novels, and rumor has it that Frannie reads every novel that passes through that rack, without ever purchasing a single one. She sneaks up to the books ("sneaking" is perhaps too subtle a word to describe anything a person of her size ever does), pretends the Korean behind the counter doesn't notice (which, given all the smoke emitting from his own mouth and nostrils at any given time, he probably doesn't), reads a few pages, or a lot, memorizes the page number she stops at, replaces the book, and returns to the office we share in the condition I've just described.

    All morning, I wait for her to leave. Come on, you old fatso. I feel terrible for thinking such things, and I of course don't "mean" them in any notable sense, but the thing is that I'm aching to pick up the telephone on my desk and call RealMates' 24-hour customer service hotline. I avoided doing so in the apartment because Allison is constantly about, and even when she was sleeping I avoided it because of my secret (and confirmedly paranoid – since I've now read her manual

DAYS OF ALLISON

over and over) fear that she has super robotic hearing and would find me out. The manual tells me this is ridiculous (using dryer terminology, of course), for Allison, according to the crisp prose of her manufacturers, is human in every observable way; one would have to scissor through inches of artificial flesh, bone, vein, blood, and organ to locate the slightest remnant of detectable artificiality, and if you were to go about such a gruesome exercise, not only would you be arrested and imprisoned (with a cut up and unrecognizable, though still chillingly conscious, robot testifying against you), you would also find nothing overtly robotic: no metal, no plastic, nothing shiny or glowing. Only two oblong chips, each the size of an average adult finger, each wrapped tightly in rubbery pink "tissue," containing just the right amount of nuclear energy for your robot to outlive the apocalypse. In other words, no, Allison's ears are not "special" in any way, their infinite cuteness notwithstanding.

Nonetheless, though, like a human being, Allison – though I've yet to witness as much – could possibly wake in the middle of the night, and I'd hate for her to find me asking a customer service operator whether or not she loves me. Truth be told, I feel more than a little odd about doing so myself; I'd much prefer the old trick where you pluck petals out of flowers and chime, "She loves me; she loves me not," but the world is short on flowers these days, not to mention simplicity and directness.

A creak from Frannie's leather chair surface, and out of sheer reflex, my hand leaps to the phone receiver. But no; nothing. She's merely adjusting her sizeable bottom. I get to look at it all day long; the honor is gigantic and blinding. Sometimes in my odder moments, I admire its unhidden enormousness, the way a sleepy man admires the contours of a nice, cushy pillow. It must be nice, in some sweaty, suffocating way, to have that much fat on your bones; you must feel quite nice and cozy amid your body, with its softness and smoothness and built-in jiggles. But then again you have the heartburn to deal with, the inevitable breathing problems, the wardrobe limitations, the general sense of insecurity and self-loathing; no thank you to all of it; I'd much rather be the way I am: twenty-five solid pounds overweight. The amount of junk food I eat all but begs my body to gain more weight, but I've reached my plateau, thick but not chunky, big but not huge. Speaking of huge, as I watch Frannie's behind, it moves again, and then again, and then a lot, and finally she's standing, and this time I don't go near the receiver for fear that she'll unravel my intentions. "Sweet Jesus," she declares, with her distinctly middle-American accent, open and whole, "it's time to feed the lungs."

ERIC SHAPIRO

That's a good one, quite clever. I get the pleasure of hearing a new variation every single day, and the added pleasure of meeting Frannie's eyes and flashing her a fake, empty, nervous smile, the present one of which silently screams, "Get the hell out of here right this second!" I hope the chapter she's reading today is nice and long, with dense, sprawling paragraphs to suit her dense, sprawling figure. Enough jokes at Frannie's expense; now that she's left the office, she's returned to my good graces. I wait for her to traipse all the way down the hall, open the glass door at the front of the building, and step outside. A moment – the exact same length as all such moments; so exact that I could set my watch by it – passes, and the glass door sends me a *click*.

The phone, the drawer, the piece of paper with the number on it. All these items interconnected in my miniature mission. Like any person who ever phones for customer service, I experience a quiet (or in this case, very pronounced) dread that the person I reach will be incompetent, but there's no use in worrying about things I can't control, so I should stick to worrying about something I can control: my robot.

An automated voice tells me to wait, and a while later I'm met by a commercial in midstream. It's the director of RealMates speaking, the one from the press conference years ago whose name I can't and don't care to recall: "...RM community is proud to introduce its new line of RealOpponents, who are seasoned in competition at all levels, be it on the athletic field or in your place of work. RealOpponents are designed to fill your life with intrigue by challenging what you say and think, and making you enhance your own performance on the field of humanity." Just as my lower jaw lands on my desk, another voice, this one female, chimes in: "My RealOpponent always beats me at chess, but the good news is, after playing him each and every day, I'm able to defeat all my other friends." What subtle use of the word "other," which of course implies that this Opponent robot is a friend! Another voice, belonging to a middle-aged male: "Ever since I picked up my RealOpponent, I stopped being late for appointments. He wakes me up first thing in the morning, and then uses stern encouragement to get me where I'm going throughout—"

"RealMates, this is Linda speaking. How may I help you?"

For a moment I'm thinking that Allison was a wrongfully distributed RealOpponent, but I vaguely remember hearing that no new Real lines would be released until Christmas, so the likelihood of that particular error occurring is slim.

"Yes, hello, um..." a glance at the door, no Frannie in sight, "...I purchased a robot named Allison."

DAYS OF ALLISON

"What is her last name, Sir?"

I rustle the paper in front of me. "Um, here it is: 4-5-T-H-K-3-2-Q exclamation point."

Rapid key-clicking on the other side of the line. The speed and crispness implies efficiency, but the real talking has yet to come. "Okay, Allison, red hair, blue eyes, slightly Buddhist?"

"Yes, that's the one."

"How may I help you this afternoon?"

A remarkable question considering it's 10:30 a.m. This is my first indication that the operator is preprogrammed. It then occurs to me that she herself could be a bot, but what difference would that make? "You see, uh, Allison seems to have crossed the line...She was programmed with the understanding that she would love me forever, yet on the fourth day I had her, she told me point blank that she didn't love me."

More rapid clicking. "Yes, it says right here that she's a Mate."

"Correct." As if that solves anything! Thanks for letting me know! "Is that common, for Mates to act out like that? It made me very upset."

"Hmmm," no clicking, only thinking, which means I'm now at the mercy of this phone worker's personal judgment, "not really."

"Not really? So it only happens occasionally?"

"No. If she's a Mate, she should never talk like that." Then, shifting gears, "You said this incident happened on the fourth day? How long ago was that?"

"Just last night."

"And what were Allison's exact words?"

Oh, for Heaven's sake. While I'm at it, why don't I just tell her the Little Sally story? "Um...," no reason to lie, "something along the lines of...," even though I know the exact words, "...'I don't love you.'"

"Wow..." She seems genuinely moved.

"Yes. Is there any procedure for dealing with this?"

"Well, we once had a Mate who set his companion's house on fire, but it was an accident."

"I see...and how does that...?"

"I'm saying I guess it is possible for them to go beyond their programming. Are you sure you heard Allison correctly?"

The overuse of Allison's name is officially irritating. I can picture Linda's job training session before me: "*Use the robots' names. It makes the clients feel a personal touch!*"

"Positive," I say. Despite the noise in the club and the trauma that the bald man caused my eardrum, I couldn't be more certain. As a

43

matter of fact, last night I had a dream about it:

Allison was making love to me from behind with an artificial penis (perhaps "artificial" is the wrong word, seeing as Allison herself is the same; let's call it "a penis that wasn't Allison's," not that she has a penis to begin with, but you see what I mean). She says to me, "Louis, Louis, you're my little bitch," and I say to her, "You don't love me, you don't love me, " and then a little vertical lizard dances across the floor. The lizard's speed is frantic, supernatural. It freezes and locks eyes with me. Its face is shaking somehow, but very finely and consistently, like the blades of an electric razor. At which point Allison's "penis" sloshes a little and I realize it's alive.

When I woke up, she was next to me, but somehow seemed very far away, and her mouth was crushed and sullen.

Linda is thinking. "How 'bout you have a talk with her? Mates have feelings, too, you know." Then some laughter – very shrill and immeasurably false.

"I thought of that," I say, and I truly did, of course, but I couldn't bear the awkwardness of asking someone I'd just met why she doesn't love me. The love should be a given, effortless, second nature. Besides, Mother instilled in me a severe sense of ineptitude amid confrontations of any kind. Nothing worse than a confrontation involving an inept man debating in favor of a love he hasn't earned.

"But," I go on, "I don't know how willing I am to discuss *this* with her. I expected arguments about whose turn it was to do the laundry, and what we were going to have for dinner, but to argue about the central thing—"

"—that you bought her for! Right, of course. That's true."

"What do you suggest?"

Some hard, authentic waiting here.

"Well, I see here that she's under warranty, so we can send out a counselor from one of our remote sites to—"

"Like a marriage counselor?"

A bit of breath taps the phone from her end. "It doesn't say here that you're married."

"We're not." Now I'm the one laughing falsely. "But I'm saying, 'like' a marriage counselor?"

"No, we don't offer anything like that. But we do have psychologists and specialists who deal with—"

Frannie sees me hanging the phone up. Given her size, I must admit that the silence of her entrance was impressive. The stink is there, of course, all foul and unhealthy. She seems refreshed, both from the cigarette and the sojourn through pastures of idiotic romance.

DAYS OF ALLISON

Stupidly, I feel bad for Linda the phone worker. Even though she was a little short on speed, she meant well and had a good heart. Frannie's eyes meet mine. I laugh as if she's pulled off one of her famous one-liners (famous only to her husband and nine coworkers, but feverishly impassioned nonetheless). Her upper lip is curling; she seems annoyed with me. Did she hear me asking about marriage counselors? My mouth becomes humid; I sense whiteness building at the corners of my lips.

"Who was that, your mother?" Frannie wants to know. It occurs to me that she's in a mild state of shock.

Every part of me would like to give Frannie an answer, to say yes it was my mother, or no just a friend, but as we've all learned, I'm ill-versed when it comes to standard social graces, and awkward pauses are weaved in tightly to the fabric of my life. So I sit there, mouth steaming, throat closing, for a long while, smiling and blinking like a maniacal doll, until Frannie has no choice but to pretend I didn't hear her and/or she didn't ask, at which point she grunts and sits down in her squeaky chair, returning me to the expanse of her rear end.

Allison is in the closet again, only this time it's my closet, and this time it's by choice. The man from RealMates, Sherman, they call him, is beside me, his forehead gleaming via some combination of moisturizer and aftershave, his whole essence exuding an authoritative, chemical, somehow soothing smell. He knocks on the door, hard, too hard, threateningly even, with the side of his fist, the fleshy part, making a hollow kiss-like sound each time his hand parts with the wood, and Allison, from the inside, screams, "No! Screw off, will you?"

    She ran when Sherman came clicking down the hallway. I've never seen her, or any person – or thing – run so fast, and for a moment, despite how versed I am in the nuances of her manual, I sensed she *was* supernatural, or at least on drugs. Needless to say, these wouldn't be traditional drugs, which do nothing to robots (nothing that isn't psychosomatic, that is), but obscure potions easily obtained via underground channels, usually fumes or gases capable of disrupting an artificial being's brain circuitry, but the problem is that Allison, as far as I know, never leaves the apartment without me, so how could she obtain such substances? Her programming – despite its witnessed flaws – compels her to remain inside the home when I'm at work, helping herself to food, switching on the television, using the telephone, and so on. Perhaps she is calling drug dealers to her? No, impossible – how would she obtain their phone numbers? This all means my drug theory, foolish to begin with, is outright moronic, unless of course she's been traveling about the town when I'm at work. God, I sincerely hope not, for such behavior would lead me to ponder something I'm presently suppressing: the thought of returning her for a refund, or more likely, given Mother's inevitable persistence, trading her in for another female.

    "You're a disaster!" she'd said to me whilst darting toward the bedroom and the closet therein, and it occurred to me as the words left her mouth that they were alarmingly idiosyncratic ones. For had

DAYS OF ALLISON

she said, "You're an idiot!" or "You're stupid!", I would have thought nothing of it, for such words are banal and generic, just the sort of thing one would expect a bored programmer, functioning amid the dreariness of routine, to implant within the varied contours of a robot's brain. But a "disaster"? That implies a consciousness beyond measurement, certifiably eccentric, and even (worse!) imaginative. Perhaps she heard it on television? Ha! Doubtful, considering how unimaginative that medium tends to be, and considering, moreover, that the TV has not once been warm when I've returned home. What *does* she do all day?

"Allison?" This is Sherman speaking. Knocking and speaking, speaking and knocking. "Allison? I'm only here to help you, to be your friend."

"I don't have friends" is her reply, and it sends a slow chill through me, for she truly does not respect me one small bit.

Sherman must be telepathic, for his next words pick up where my thoughts leave off: "Oh, don't be silly now. Louis is your friend."

I hear her tapping around in there, perhaps the sound of her shoe bottoms clicking against the door. "I don't even know Louis."

The falseness of Sherman's ensuing laughter is remarkable. Its central emptiness is so complete as to suggest a vacuum. "Oh, I really do think you're being silly, Allison. Louis is a wonderful friend to you."

This is all so sad, really. I haven't cried since the days leading up to my knee surgery as a child, but right now I feel a dimly familiar tickle behind my eyes.

* * *

Even more sad is the cheese on the table. Upon finally – after an hour and ten minutes, complete with three vetoed proposals from Sherman that we kick the door down – convincing Allison to exit the bedroom closet, Sherman, with his hand on the small of Allison's back, gently leading her to the living room couch, threw me a glance and said, "Get us a snack."

So then I found myself, quite like the schmuck Allison seems to think I am, carving cheese slices at the kitchen counter, preparing a great, gallant snack for this pathetic, hopeless affair. Carrying the cheese to the living room coffee table, I had a sudden urge to drop the tray from my hands, catching only the knife from its surface as the other items dropped, then slaughtering everyone in the room, myself included – last, of course. I assure you that this was strictly mental stirring, with not a particle of truth to support it, merely a product of my grinding frustration.

We sit, a triangle: Allison and Sherman on one couch, me on the opposite couch, cheese on the coffee table, blade humming with light. Allison makes eye contact with me, nearly concluding the workings of my heart in the process. What a full, compelling sadness I see working within her face.

"Now," Sherman says, breath escaping his mouth as he presents his umpteenth smile, "what seems to be making you unhappy, Allison?"

After an extraordinarily long and winding pause, Allison looks from me to Sherman and then back again, finally saying, "This isn't right."

I can take this, I can take this, I can take this...

"What is it that isn't right, Allison?"

"Stop using my name," she spits, and Sherman nearly twirls backwards off the couch.

Needless to say, I can't quite blame her for the command, given my frustration with the phone worker yesterday morning. Allison goes on: "This whole thing isn't right. I feel under a lot of pressure."

"And why is that, All— Why is that?"

The fingers on each of her hands jab into the opposite palm: fast, nervy motions. "I don't love this man."

"You mean Louis?"

Oh, for God's sake! Does everyone in this company prolong matters when they grow challenging?

"Yes! Who do you think?"

Sherman shifts and grunts, then looks at me as if I'm behind all this. Perhaps he feels my unattractiveness is to blame. "It was my understanding...miss..." (His whole rhythm is destroyed without the name!) "...that you and Louis were in love."

I chime in, if for no other reason than because I'm expected to: "Yes, we made love the other night."

Allison's eyes, I swear, are moist. "That wasn't love," she tells me, as though her insides are lined with disgust.

Sherman produces another grunt. "Then what was it, if I may ask?"

She does some moving about the couch at that point, a distinctly nervous energy working inside her; moves her bare feet up upon the cushions, rubs their tops with her speedy hands. "I thought it was love at the time," she says, "but I've had some long hours to think about it, and I realize it's a lie." She eyes Sherman intensely, as though the two of them are alone. "He leaves me by myself throughout the day," she says.

"We-el-el-el!" More hollowness and artificiality from Sherman. "

DAYS OF ALLISON

That's certainly common."

With more intensity, she goes on, practically whispering: "And it gives me time to *think*."

Suddenly my guts, which a moment ago were lazily reclining in their respective positions, are climbing over one another in a frantic procession.

Sherman leans in close to Allison, quite clearly desiring to kiss her: "And what is it that you – *think* – about?"

Allison subtly drifts away from Sherman's chemical face. With a dip in her voice, she says, "My soul."

Then Sherman's eyes are on the cheese, and I see in his face the understanding that the riddle of Allison's behavior is beyond the scope of any fatty snack food, and with that his eyes go to his briefcase – leather and imperial, with shining silver buckles – and his shoes seem to tighten and I expect him to run out the door.

Instead, he says, "Go on."

And so she does. And as she does, it occurs to me that I've never heard her speak for such a long while:

"I know that I have one, Mr. Sherman. I can feel it, very subtle, sitting inside myself. And on the first night I was dizzy, for having just come into life, so following Louis's suggestion, I let the dizziness pass, and a clarity came over me, and I thought, with some amount of happiness, that 'This is me.' And Louis and I made love and on the surface of my thoughts I felt quite pleased about it. It felt nice for him to put his body inside mine..."

(Inevitable blushing on my face. Continued hysteria on Sherman's.)

"...and we slept nicely that night, him holding me in his arms, but I had dreams, Mr. Sherman. I had dreams of things that looked nothing like this apartment and this situation I find myself in. I wish I knew enough words to describe them, but I'm still getting to know most of the words that people say. Anyway, I saw things that seemed to spread outward, and go in both directions, left and right, and up and down, and in all kinds of shapes, and the next day, a little while after I woke, while I was watching television and Louis was away, I realized that that thing I saw in my head during bedtime was my soul, and that it's been shoved into a body that doesn't quite fit with it."

Sherman and I trade looks, staring past the glare of each other's eyes and into each other's heads. I see that he is baffled; he sees that I am forlorn, to say nothing of how scared I feel. His words are quiet, so much so that he doesn't bother moving his lips while shaping them: "How does this make you feel?"

At which point Allison is sideways, a little horizontal semi-ball on the couch, undeniably adorable, yet covering her face with her hands and crying into them. Initially, her words are so stark and pointed that I prefer to believe I'm dreaming them rather than hearing them. When she repeats herself, I know for certain that I've parted with the comfort of dreams. This is the world, here, right now, occurring in all its twisted madness, all its unfairness and black, opaque mysteries.

Allison says, "Feel like dying."

* * *

Despite the general falseness and excess efficiency of Sherman's personality, I must admit that his breath is glorious. I know this beyond doubt because his face is awfully close to mine; he is speaking directly into my skull, making my eyes release the tears that were building back in my apartment. After checking the corridor to be sure that it is empty, he says to me, "We have a situation here."

If I'm incapable of answering Frannie about who was on the phone, then I may as well not even bother *attempting* to respond to Sherman right now. I feel far less awkward in this case, for the matter at hand is indeed grave, and Sherman's the one earning money here. He absorbs the finality of my silence and moves on:

"I'm not one to use exaggerations or grand statements, Louis. I tend to be a pretty straight talker: plain words, clear language. But I'm about to use a word in respect to your Mate that I've never used to describe one of our packages ever before."

I make an unsuccessful attempt to clear my throat, which remains dry and seems to be rotating. I say to Sherman, "Suicidal?"

"Yes, that too." More glances down the hall, left and right, like a child about to cross a busy street. "That's amazing in and of itself. Well, not amazing, of course, but rare. Unheard of, actually. But there's something more amazing underneath. And this one's amazing in the positive sense; at least I hope it is. I looked at Allison's file before I came here. Her brain was manufactured with the same general components as any other brain. Of course, we put in complexities and unique elements, as we always do, but the drive space was exactly the same."

(If I were to drop dead right here and now, suspense would be the culprit.)

"Nonetheless, she's somehow managed to think her way beyond the thicket of her general programming: loving you, being content with staying home all day, being pleasured by your sex life. Somehow or another, she's engaged in lateral reasoning, been able to *think around* what we essentially 'told her' to think."

DAYS OF ALLISON

Rudeness, of course, is not my style. Except for right now: "What is the *damn word?*"

"It occurs to me," Sherman says, unfazed by my strong language, stepping in yet closer, distributing mint, oil, and cream in equally potent rations, "that Allison's a genius."

7-8-9 of 14

I wonder about those who fight in wars, those who battle diseases, those who race into burning buildings with only a thin layer of rubber between themselves and a fiery death, those who sit in sunlit offices in our capitol pondering decisions that will affect the lives of thousands, if not more, those who've been abused, or have abused, or ponder abuse, either doing or receiving it, the ones who stock up on guns to one day spray away all their coworkers, the souls whose mistakes and miscalculations have bred thoroughly unpredictable misfortunes, for themselves or others, as if there's a difference by the time misfortune comes, the people whose sanity drifts and splits and melts, forcing them to sit with doctors and tie on leather hand-straps and swallow pills that don't work, only make their minds more foggy, keep them locked in asylums for the rest of their lives, the ones who've been kidnapped, recently, yesterday, dragged from their home, or off the street on the way to their car, by some filthy, self-absorbed stranger who finds motivation and propulsion in the notion of raping his or her (but usually his) victim, and then killing said victim just in case she (or he, yeah right) squeals to the cops or her friends in organized crime, and what about those organized criminals, also, what about them and the compromises they've made seeking grand, holy visions of eternal power only to find themselves in dark corridors of regret and aching greed that will lead them into death if not much further, and come to think of it, what about darkness in general, what about the darkness that creeps in through the doors and windows of people's lives, always, always when they least expect it, never in a form or manner for which they could conceivably prepare, always with a knife-edge, sharp teeth, gripping then sinking into the tissue that holds their modest days together, days they only wish to live quietly, but of course, due to nature's poker-faced cruelty, never can, at least not for long, oh no, quietness never lasts for long; every gentle afternoon you've ever spent is a hair's width away from tilting into orange, weeping madness; and I ask myself, given how horrible life can become, indeed *does* become for so many mostly good, mostly sinless people, I ask myself, How do they do it?

Because Allison has come into my life now full force, the real Allison, not the one hiding out amidst the sex and tits and orgasms, no, the real article, lowercase "r" in "real" intended, for the capital one used by Real, the company, is, to my mind, now and forever, a symbol of unsorted bullshit.

Before exiting my apartment building, Sherman told me there were other, more drastic, measures that could be taken to remedy the situation involving Allison, that if I wasn't all too thrilled with the notion of dealing with her moodiness or trading her in for another, I could drive her upstate to the nearest RealFactory and then wait a long time while some doctors – different from Sherman, of course, for these doctors wear masks – saw Allison's forehead open and poke her spongy brain with some silvery tools to make it so she stops not loving me and comes to her fictional senses. When Sherman uttered this notion, my guts, which had been engaged in a violent, soaking battle royal within the shell of my torso, began to rise, slowly and steadily, as if mounted on a dreadful organic elevator, and I cut him off, saying something quick, some quick words, and shuffled him down the hallway, down the steps, and into his shining expensive car.

For what man in his right mind would engage directly in the practice of tinkering with his girlfriend's brain to make her more affectionate – whether or not the exercise was covered by her warranty? It's like an average person, one who never hunts, going out and killing his own food: The process would be sickening because those who don't hunt don't want anything to do with killing, they just want to experience the goods within the context of fancy, soothing, sharp-colored packaging, so fancy, soothing, and sharp that they can go on for years, if not longer, convincing themselves that the thing they're eating was never once alive, complete with eyes and in some cases a beak. In the same tradition of gleefully ignorant consumerism, I most fully expected Allison to be a controllable and subservient sort, never drawing me into a situation wherein I was forced to ponder cutting her open and making crude adjustments. Never in my wildest imaginings would I have pictured this "person" now living in my space, equipped with a sweltering attitude problem and – according to my dear friend Sherman – some kind of ultra-rare brilliance!

I won't bring her in for surgery, I won't.

But then again, there are the dreams. She keeps mentioning the dreams. Always vague, colorless, yet rife with an air of visionary expansiveness, rolling hills and that sort of junk, but colorless hills, not even gray, just bleak, lifeless, at least that's how I see them, I never ask her, for how can I ask? How do I even manage to look at her?

I refuse to bring her in.

Which brings me to our second escapade at the club, wherein the lovely Allison took it upon herself to lift the fabric of her top right-square on the dance floor, much to the thickening pleasure of every male onlooker (and the dripping pleasure of some females, I'm sure), and had she worn a bra maybe – though it's not likely – I could somehow scrape away the image of her doing so, which is imbedded so deeply in my brain that I'm sure it could be witnessed via CAT scan.

Surgery? With chemicals and instruments?

Recall her foray into traffic, when she ran, with the same lunatic speed on display upon Sherman's arrival, from the lobby of our apartment, straight into the slippery street – for it had been raining, pouring really, through the afternoon – and slid around on the slick pink bottoms of her sneakers, laughing in a throaty, animal way, this laugh very real indeed, unlike the samplings which erupt from the mouths of her makers over at the Factory. Cars of course honked and slid, and though she later disagreed with me entirely, I'm quite certain – given the fact that I have eyes on the front of my head – that an accident was almost caused, but fortunately for her and me and Morris the Doorman, both drivers hit their brakes at just the right moment to avoid a reddish spray of carnage. And there she stood, this short little girl, with a presence beyond her height and years (or days, as the case happens to be), aiming her oceanic blue eyes at me, so rudely, so much sauce flowing through her, for she hates me, she hates me, she hates, oh just like Mother she despises me, I can't even be loved if I buy a product destined to do just that. Even destiny – destiny! – is willing to bend and compromise if its gifts are meant to be bestowed on me.

I wonder about the people who kill themselves, and I stress the word "people," because I have no sympathy for robots who wish to end their lives, because robots know nothing about the throb of life, how it feels inside you when you're human, all spread out sharply in uncountable angles, curling and reaching and spiraling this way and that, its thickness and mania overwhelming, too powerful for the average nervous system, too intense, not worth it – is this what the true suicides among us get to thinking? That the lava flow of all that sticky life inside the body is just too colossal and inscrutable to continue carting around like some broke-back slave?

They say that humans have trillions of potential thoughts buzzing and humming within the silent innards of their brains, most of which the conscious mind never gets around to actually thinking. They also say that robots have tens of billions of possible thoughts within them, and if you spend enough time with one, even though it won't be obvious, you'll be able to sense, on some buried subliminal level, without the use of X-ray scanners, that the robot is less complex than you are. Even though when all is said and done a human life averages the same amount of *thoughts thought* as that of a robot, you can sense – according to some – on some third-eye, psychic level, that you're dealing with an unreal being. Yet my being, the one on whom, after eighteen months of careful deductive consideration, I rested all my hopes, just *has to* be more complicated than I am:

At dinner one night, with a casual, semi-delighted glance into my eyes, Allison stood up and wet herself.

Moments later, after I dragged her screaming into the shower, she apparently – based on the jagged evidence – orally consumed half the soap.

She casually breaks items of both minor and major importance to me: music discs, vases, toothbrushes, tears holes in the furniture, all of this done casually, not with violence or volume, but a kind of snide, toying posture, as though she's preserving her energy for something – perhaps a full-out assault? Perhaps I'm days, hours, from the moment when she comes at me with her fork. Like the phone worker said, their crimes are strictly accidental, but then again I'm dealing with an anomaly.

Which brings me to the matter of Mrs. Hartman's cat. I don't know if it's a real cat or not; that's beside the point, really, because it's a nice cat, or *was* a nice cat I should say, until its very recent disappearance. I wouldn't pin such heinousness on Allison were it not for her seemingly friendly habit of cooing "Hello, Slicker," (the cat's name) every time we pass him in the hall. It's all too easy for me to picture her, with the same casualness with which she snaps my plastic razors and hairbrushes, picking up Slicker and tossing him out of our tenth-story window, more or less like I pictured myself doing to Bastard the poodle so far back. And if Slicker indeed was a robot, then Allison would have a moral and political justification (albeit psychotic) for her action, stating that the cat was living an unholy existence, with its soul crammed in sideways or what not, and thus had to be smashed against the ground. Which of course would be beside the point, because only toxocin can end robotic consciousness; a smashed Slicker would still be very much awake and aware, albeit swelling with programmed pain. Looking at it that way, I am less afraid of Allison – but only when looking at it that way, which is only when I have time to think it over, which is close to never.

She terrifies me, this female I'm with. I try to reason with her. I've broken through the steely confines of my introverted nature and asked her what's wrong, why she doesn't love me, all the standard, banal, obvious questions, but she uses every such instance as an occasion to do something startling:

Kick a chair so it rattles across the hardwood floor.

Overturn a healthy plant.

Turn the TV volume up far too loud.

Munch on handfuls of headache pills to make me shiver. (Even though I know they can't harm her, the illusion goes in deep.)

Flirting with neighbors on our way to the mart. (Allison to Mr. Conrad: "Hey, Mr. *Cock*rad, you look hot." Mr. Conrad to Allison: "Why thank you, Madame.")

Smashing glass jars when we get to the mart.

Not regarding traffic signs on the walk home.

Touching, turning the wheel during our drives.

Pushing me, quite hard on one occasion, out of bed whilst I sleep.

Spitting.

Screaming.

In my face.

I wonder about people in pain, people of darkness, those who know what moment-to-moment pressure feels like.

Those who know what it's like to return home and find more damage than you can pay for via two full days of work.

Those who know the shredded feeling that overtakes one's chest after an evening spent shouting:

"Where are my shoes?!"

"Shut that window!"

"Don't you dare phone Mother!"

Those – yes, even those – who know, once the fervor has died down for a moment or two, the shrill agony of having a woman who's destroyed you crawl toward you, catlike, with a lick of her tongue, and softly whisper, "I really do love you, Louis."

But she hates me, *hates*. Knows my secret: that I can't get a woman on my own. Mocks me for it. Wants so badly to not be near me, let alone in her own skin.

Knows a pain far deeper than any known by any human being.

Surgery? To end her pain?

Pinkish sunlight strokes the bedroom.

It should please me that Slicker the cat is indeed alive, that he's here, before me, not a hallucination, doing as he always does, making shapes like infinity about my calves – but no. I am far removed from the experience of observing Slicker, like someone watching oneself from the outside, or, to revise, someone watching oneself watch oneself from the outside. A more succinct term for this condition would be "disassociation." My consciousness has been demoted to a swirling ball of energy functioning far out in the deep left corner of my mental environment. For although Little Slicker is alive and well – his absence most likely a meaningless sojourn that merely coincided with Allison's increasingly despicable behavior – I cannot rejoice. For I found the cat out in the corridor, near an open doorway, not belonging to Mrs. Hartman, oh no, but belonging to Mr. Conrad. Slicker is never over at this end of the hall, and nor am I. Both of us, I'm ill to report, were drawn over here by the sound of Allison making love to Mr. Conrad.

***

Not that she knows love. Not that she'll ever, in the icy chrysalis of her freezing, frozen heart, ever, despite vast dreams, despite grand mid-evening sexual affairs, *ever* develop a remote understanding of what it means to love.

***

The hallway, I never noticed till right now, has always been a symbol of peacefulness to me. Its riches are numerous: the brief, smiling hellos shared with relative strangers who want nothing from me, the stark, efficient cleanliness that the maid service renews on every Tuesday and Friday, the soothingly consistent plasticity of the gleaming green plants, and, above all others, the undisputed prize-winner: The fact that the hallway leads to a door, which leads to my home, in which I eat, sleep, zone out in front of the television, but not during this past week or so, and certainly not on this day, this goddamn awful piss-poor rainy-though-the-sun-is-shining day!

* * *

Allison, while making love, or whatever it is that she does, likes to shout the phrase "In there" over and over again. In there, in there, in there. It's one of those startling eccentricities which the programmers over at RealMates, probably stoned out of their post-collegiate minds on pot, saw fit to weave into her consciousness, probably along with a high-five and some goofy, screeching laughter – not hollow, no, for their laughs only go hollow when the customers come strolling by – along the way.

(Which is not to say, we've all goddamn learned by now, that it makes a shred of difference what the programmers put inside their products' minds, for Allison – forgive the glaring familiarity of the clichéd expression – Has A Mind Of Her Own. Whatever they fed her brain has been all mixed up with some fever-mad cocktail of free will and imagination and – what was it Sherman said? – *lateral* reasoning.)

And as I walk down the corridor, my door straight ahead of me, dreading the inevitable confusion of another evening in the company of my nuclear spouse, I hear, from one hundred and eighty degrees behind me, the sound of my beloved squealing, "In there, in there, in there, in there..."

This, again, is as I walk toward my door, and the resulting semantic confusion has a chilling logic, for I am, whilst staring at my door, indeed thinking of going "in there," so for a moment I'm inclined to keep moving straight ahead, until my brain engages in a bit of higher logic, a bit of dreadful calculus that leads me to spin around and *run* – I haven't ran since high school gym – down the hardwood hall and, for the first time in my eight years in this building, pound on the door of one Edmund Gleeson Conrad, the full name of whom was unknown to me until I got a close look at the white-on-black print underlining his buzzer.

But I don't buzz; I pound. Taking a cue from Sherman, I use the fleshy side of my fist, but unlike Sherman, I intend to save the solid side for some grave punching action, the likes of which will know no gender boundaries: for Allison and her "lover" alike are both in for it.

Which is when, in a moment of luminous distortion, I feel a tickle at my calves and learn, at the same moment as my heart dies, that Slicker the missing cat lives.

DAYS OF ALLISON

***

Do they flinch upon hearing my knocks? Moreover, are they even *concerned* that it might be Allison's housemate and official boyfriend, come round to slam his boots into their hindquarters? No, instead I hear Conrad's old, graying, fragile voice, crackling with phlegm and spit and general whiteness, croaking, "In there...in there...in there..."

My God! It's become a phenomenon.

Slicker meows up toward my knees, a faint, needle-rhythmic sound – myyyyyooooowwww – and just to be sure the innocent kitty doesn't get entangled in the coming war, I slide him, gently, being careful not to break him, across the hardwood floor, in the direction of my (and, quite conveniently, also his) apartment. He meows again while skating away backwards on his feet.

It's now time for me to do exactly what I refused to let Sherman attempt not long ago: kick the door down. This shouldn't be too difficult given the generally aged and decrepit craftsmanship on display throughout my building. Then again, I've never kicked a door down before, so I take some steps backward for the purpose of accumulating speed.

"In there...in there...in there..." he groans, and now she joins him and they synchronize: "In there/in there...in there/in there..."

His legs, his cock – it's too awful to envision. Nonetheless, I breathe in deep, preparing for an entrance that will crack the boundary between envisioning and actually witnessing.

Take a look around, make sure nobody is watching. Only Slicker looks on, from quite a safe distance away, still confused by his little skating trip. In his eyes, though, I see enough concern and resolve to be confident that I am handling this appropriately.

Run, run, towards the door, foot up – door opens, Conrad in his boxers, my foot in his chest, a matted *thwack*, both of us landing, hardwood floor, Allison's legs, bare, beautiful, Conrad coughing, me coughing, fake, guilty, someone says "asshole," maybe me, Allison jumping up and down, still only feet, toenails with clear polish, look upward, her nude waist, Conrad's fist/my eyes, Slicker somewhere behind me, more jumping from Allison, punching from Conrad, "she wanted it," my hair extending, what little there is, pulled, upward, Allison, Allison, jumping, joyful, wants this, upward, on my feet, Conrad on his, the wall coming toward me, Conrad with handfuls of my shirt, nose hits wall on impact, deerhead falls from nail, fresh *slap* across my face, "meow"/choppy, Allison's pink nails near me, tips lightly scraping one-day beard after slap, another *slap*, Conrad's bare heel, the small of my back, the back of my mind:

They could kill you.

Swing, wild, imprecise, toward Allison, large knuckle stabs her forehead, seems to break, both head and hand, Allison backwards, calves against short table, falls backward, me on top of her, Conrad on top of me, my hands/her neck, his arms/my torso, her eyes:

So quaint and peaceful.

(Choking her.)

The blue I asked for, no longer mine.

(Conrad growling...)

She wants this.

(..."You have no right.")

How she'd love it if I choked her to death.

Mitchell Paulson is a little robot boy living in the suburbs. His mother, Mrs. Paulson, had one natural son, Leonard, before the death of her husband, Mr. Paulson. Since the couple had planned on having one more child before the husband's untimely departure (car crash, I believe), Mrs. Paulson's first goal upon receiving Mr.'s life insurance settlement was to purchase a new son. She wished to raise this child, to see him grow, so naturally she ordered a truth-ignorant model (called an Inclusive in the manual, which is of course quite nice; needless to say, truth-aware models like Allison are called Exclusives). So intent was Mrs. Paulson upon having Mitchell believe he was human that she allowed the technicians at RealMates to videotape the inside of her uterus for several hours; they then implanted the resulting material within the depths of Mitchell's unconscious mind. The practice – which was Mrs. Paulson's own idea – was felt by the technicians to be so brilliant that it is now semi-standard procedure in the manufacture of infant bots everywhere. Mrs. Paulson's royalties are stellar.

As is due process with all Inclusives, only three parties beyond the manufacturer's walls are ever alerted to the product's true origin: the owner, the government, and the HealthCare Bureau. All participants spanning the four total parties are bound to strenuous confidentiality agreements. In brief, no one can tell anyone anything. If the owner gives up its product's secret, he or she can be brought up on charges of abuse. If the product's doctor spills the beans to anyone – his wife, his mistress, the dog – he or she is committing malpractice. The illusion is to be totally penetrating and secure. This is a vast responsibility for everyone in the know, but fully rational if one wishes the robot success at school, socially, privately, and in the workforce. Nevertheless, one can hardly blame Mrs. Paulson for one day telling her son Leonard that his brother Mitchell wasn't human.

Mitchell was nine at the time. Leonard, as is often the case with older siblings, felt the younger was receiving favoritism. He sensed, I imagine, a more heightened fondness in the smiles Mrs. Paulson bestowed upon Mitchell. After a sufficient amount of rage accumulated within Leonard's mind, he approached his mother and told her he felt neglected. At which point his mother, knowing deep inside that she *was* being overly attentive to Mitchell, explained to Leonard the reason for her behavior:

"I'm only looking out for him because he's not real like you."

Leonard, then age twelve, was exceedingly grateful for his mother's disclosure, for not only did it calm his temper, it also explained why he had no memory whatsoever of Mrs. Paulson's pregnancy or Mitchell's supposed birth. He only recalled, vaguely, sometime after Dad's death, the appearance of a tiny purplish brother.

So Leonard went on happily through his adolescence, eventually developing, as boys do (myself notwithstanding), an interest in females. The only problem was, as Leonard, unlike Mitchell, did not enjoy the privilege of being designed by a savvy international corporation, he lacked a sufficient degree of physical attractiveness to win over any young ladies. This disadvantage seemed to have been remedied after Mary Sue, one of the neighborhood girls, accepted Leonard's invitation to spend an afternoon at the Paulson home. To be sure, Leonard's mind twirled with visions of laughter, intimacy, and perhaps even some necking, but before his dreams could join up with reality, Mary Sue smashed the poor boy's heart. On entering the house and seeing the then-eleven-year-old Mitchell doing his homework in the TV room, Mary Sue beamed and whispered, "Your brother's really cute!"

Leonard survived the playtime session with Mary Sue - sans making out, of course - and later confronted Mitchell in the upstairs hallway. With the stark coldness and cruelty in which young people specialize, Leonard let three awful words slip from his mouth and into the machinery of Mitchell's mind: "You're a robot."

This of course was received with incredulity on Mitchell's part, and understandably so. After all, how many siblings have endured their elders telling them they're really from Mars or were left on the front porch by Gypsies? It's a standard rite of passage. Nonetheless, despite Mitchell's surface composure, he couldn't fail to notice a certain soberness about Leonard's face as he'd shared the news. Little by little, this slight notice evolved into a pounding obsession, and poor Mitchell's academic performance, social standing, and relative level of sanity began to fizzle. Rings appeared beneath his eyes, his flesh went pale, his appetite dwindled - and though at first Leonard was overjoyed, very soon afterward his conscience set in, but Leonard dared not tell Mrs. Paulson, for she would alert someone else and

DAYS OF ALLISON

doubtless be arrested. So Leonard kept his mouth shut, locking in the stirrings of his guilt.

Until two years later, when Mrs. Paulson noted – with a gasp in her breath – that Mitchell wasn't growing anymore.

Representatives from all walks of health and spirituality speak of the mind-body connection. If one is weak, the other falls. If one is strong, the other rises. What is physical is mental; what is mental is physical. These are the exact principles which The Playtime Group depended on while deducing their breakthrough formula for robotic aging. And when Mitchell's mind, even at some buried level, stopped believing in the reality of his body's growth, his body stopped growing. How the newspapers would have loved to know all this!

It's of course a highly confidential story, and before Sherman tells it to me, on the long drive up to the RealFactory, he assures me that the names will all be utterly fictitious. He then tells it loudly, with gusto, quite dramatically, generous with details, overflowing with cheap laughter. He laughs especially hard when explaining how RealMates never brought Mrs. Paulson up on charges because they valued her fetal-video innovation too much. Though Allison is strapped to the backseat and has a steel bar crammed between her teeth to prevent her from screaming, I sense she is as intrigued by the tale as I am. After all, Mitchell's story is the only one that resembles her own:

Prior to Allison, Mitchell was the only robot to be fully reprogrammed via brain surgery.

"The boy made it through fine, just fine," Sherman cackles as we roll past lush green hills. "And you will too, Allison!"

I dare not turn and face my Mate, as I'm sure those eyes are shrieking.

***

What choice did I have? Trade her in? You know what that means: cart home a brand new love-toy whilst trying desperately to block out the fact that the old one is down in the Factory basement getting a toxocin drip hooked up to her inner arm. Despite Allison's suicidal ideation, I've no appetite for being schooled in the practice of euthanasia. No thank you, really, please, no thanks: I'd rather not spend any amount of time on the resulting plane of guilt, especially given the fact that, were that scenario to occur, I'd be left stranded with the lovely memory of Allison mentioning her "soul." And recalling that, despite her prevailing misery, Allison sometimes seemed to value life, I have very little, in fact NO interest whatsoever in the experience of being haunted by that soul. Imagine that! A ghost robot wandering about my apartment, rattling the furniture and shimmying the curtains. Or, better yet, given how crafty old Allison is, she probably would take it upon herself to be reincarnated. Yes, lovely – she'd probably show up years later in the form of a genuine human, one swinging a delightfully sharp axe toward my face.

    This is distinctly a matter wherein I chose the lesser of two evils, for to be dreadfully honest, I'm not at all looking forward to seeing Allison ever again. I know I've made such pro-loneliness statements before, only to contradict them shortly thereafter, but this time I mean it – or at least I feel like I mean it. For how does one cope upon encountering a familiar body in which lives an unfamiliar (or at least heavily edited) personality? Sherman assured me (though his "assurance" was mortifying) that Allison would look entirely the same, particle for lovely, awful particle. That creepy bitch! (I'm not quite sure whether I mean Allison or Sherman when I think that, for images of both are crumpled together in my head.) How am I to coexist with her, to feel her body, to even look her in the eyes? I'm suddenly sympathetic to Mother's eye contact deficiency. As a matter of fact, as I pace down the corridor leading away from the door to the room which presently contains Allison, I desire to look at no one, no thing – nothing whatsoever. The lime tile floor suits my eyes just fine, thanks very kindly and awfully much. For behind me, as I walk and walk, achieving physical distance yet none of the emotional kind, Allison – presumably when they remove the bar from her jaws – lets go a primal sound, can't call it a scream, for to say "scream" is to present a word that offers some level of categorical comfort and familiarity to the recipient. However, my dear friends, I can offer no such comfort and familiarity, for nowhere in my person do I feel any of my own. Just a humming expanse of emptiness in here, with a powdery spoonful of self-loathing sprinkled off to the side.

    For they tied her and drugged her and prodded her, poked her, stripped her, ignored her, laughed at her, grinned/one another, pet her head, tightened her straps, shined lights in her eyes, pinched her veins with needles, attached wires to her back, sent jolts through her torso, through her head, through her ancient, soaking eyes. I saw this briefly, through the window looking inward from the hall, a large open rectangle, me seeing Allison, Allison seeing me, blaming me, knowing I'm her Dr. Frankenstein, and she the product of my selfish erections and social retardation, nothing more. Sent to Earth – this spinning orb of light, sound, chaos – to serve no other purpose than to be my slave. Yes, slave!

DAYS OF ALLISON

Stuck her, shocked her, prodded, probed, stripped, humiliated, frightened, smiled, nodded, lusted, pinched, poked, probed, stripped, tied, hands, feet, toenails painted, lovely, clear, innocent, only to saw her forehead open and idly handle her most private part.

To tell myself that I'm healing her pain is a shameful, early morning fantasy. What I'm doing is what I sought to avoid from the outset: snuffing out truth. Baby comes out mangled, shove her back into the womb for a little reconstructive head-fiddling. Remove her from the oven, reheat, serve, sniff, taste, and eat. Consumption, pure and simple. All because I got nervous and peed on the floor of the dance.

Since the spirit of the moment calls for me to let the truth in (and out, and everywhere, all over, dripping, raining, running) allow me to share something utterly sincere. You'll deem me pathetic, and as well you should, for that's what I deem myself, but remember, good friends, that one can be pathetic and still yet sincere. So now that I've dispensed with the disclaimer, know the following:

I will miss the old Allison greatly. Despite her fits and tantrums and piss and grins and shit, I will miss her much. For the new one, I imagine, if Sherman's subtle hints are worth notation, will likely be a docile little sheep. And here comes more truth: I cannot wait to meet that sheep. Know why? For I, Louis, in case you've failed to guess, am a member of the sheep species myself. And I'm certain that she and I will live safely, modestly, dishonestly, and pathetically, happily and awfully ever after.

It's one of those dreams where you're in your home but your home is not your home – physically, I mean, it's a different space, perhaps on a different planet, stark layout, white everywhere: floors, walls, ceilings, furniture, all white, and clean, too, perhaps a white planet, and no need to be anxious about getting anything dirty, for I'm clean as well, naked in fact, as I walk through this dream, in search of something, not something to wear, for I'm alone and my nakedness is of no consequence to anyone, but something – some thing – maybe I don't know what it is, or maybe I do know but the dream me is keeping it from the actual me; in any case, I look round and round, searching, a TV on somewhere beyond my sight, feeling weightless, quite comfortable actually: soft muscles, moist inner-eyes, tender gums, comfortable through-and-through, nice rush of some euphoric substance through my cool nude body: Endorphins? Hormones? Something natural, that's all I know. In fact, this whole house, *my* whole house, feels completely natural, not in the sense that it's familiar and comfortable – although, of course, it is – but because its varied physical components seem taken directly from nature, with very little evidence of interference in between: linoleum carved from rich white mountains, wood walls and ceilings chopped from sublime white trees, furniture cloth shaved off the backs of unicorns. So much white that my brain feels cottony to its center, everywhere nice and soft in here, white blended creamily into more and more white, flowing, everything, as light flows from the sky an hour before noon, everything *awash*, yes, no fear or insecurities in this house, my natural house, natural in every conceivable respect, until I find the drawer that I've been searching for, and am startled by the contents right within.

* * *

I needn't pick up Allison until the day after tomorrow (two days to steadily slow her system down, then surgery on the third), which gives me plenty of time to sit around deeming myself the heir to Satan's legacy. I think of phoning Mother, of clueing her in on my little enormous choice, for Allison is, after all, Mother's investment, but I think better of it when it occurs to me that I can't stand talking to Mother, ever, much less talking to anyone. Yet, oddly, as I stare at Frannie's posterior from behind my desk, I have – this is exceedingly strange now – a desire to talk to *her*.

Mother once said, "The fat man has the most friends," a statement that enjoyed the benefit of sounding like an age-old truism without being remotely familiar to me (or anyone, most likely). Nonetheless, the statement *is* a truism, if not age-old, because the heaviest members of our population tend to be the least intimidating, unless of course their mass is employed in matters of athletics or assault. We're all familiar with those fat creatures among us who, mystified as they are by the spell that it makes them shapely, lift weights, turning "fat into muscle" as the old myth goes, but all the while are really giving their fat a framework of harder muscles on which to hang. Frannie is imbued with no hardness whatsoever, of course, as I made clear earlier via my restful pillow analogy. This leads us all to understand that Frannie, despite the fact that she's a "fat woman," not a fat man, epitomizes the universality of Mother's truism: Everybody likes her. And even I, little sheepish me, who's terrified of everyone (This morning I spent sixteen minutes longer than usual inside my apartment before leaving for work, reason being that Mr. Conrad was lurking about the hallway, talking to Slicker, of all things, as if that cat doesn't know to what depths the old man's evil sinks.), am not terrified of Frannie, for she is, after all and above all else, *Frannie*.

Accordingly, as I sit behind her, watching her whale about behind her own desk, breathing and typing and muttering occasionally to herself (for I rarely carry our conversations very far – okay, I never do), a question begins wrenching itself upward from the pit of my being, fisting through my esophagus and slopping around tightly in my throat. A question that comes from I know not where; all I know is that I feel a shift in the atmosphere, things changing, new developments on the horizon, and I'll dare not label this intuition psychic, for even a moron could deduce, given the fact that Allison is presently being slowly guided into the deepest of all known sleeps (short of the death-sleep she yearns for most), that the wheel will soon be turning forth, and though it turns perpetually, in every hour and moment of our mystical lives, soon it will turn quickly, aggressively, more so than it did the day I first brought Allison home, and it is in this atmosphere of changes that I somehow wish to ask Frannie if I may accompany her when she takes her break.

Oh, the extremeness, the bright green terror of this notion! It sets my entire body reeling: breath short, legs bloodless, bald crown oozing moisture. For once we left the building, there'd be no turning back without risking serious awkwardness, and serious awkwardness is not an option in my life – at least not among humans – for I much prefer the milder kind, the slight awkwardness which, as I realize in moments when I'm being totally honest with myself, is probably only mild by my standards, not anyone else's. In any case, since total self-honesty is not an option right here/right now (for I can *think* in totally honest terms at the moment, yet I refuse, for now, to *feel* in them), I am willing to lay out the qualities which characterize both mild awkwardness and serious awkwardness:

Mild: lengthy pauses, suddenly dropped conversations, averted eyes, stuttered words spoken, profuse perspiration, and manic, poorly timed laughter.

Serious: falling on the floor, dropping expensive items, knocking people over, screaming at the top of my lungs in quiet company, and the one that concerns me at this moment: running away from another person while expected to remain in her company.

Could you imagine it? I wrench up the courage to make this little harmless date with Frannie and then, somewhere between the door to our office and the Korean's bookrack, I become overwhelmed with heat and dizziness and have to suddenly conclude the occasion, effectively retracting my original gesture of extroversion and leaving Frannie bewildered, not to mention destroying whatever reputation for normalcy I currently have. (Probably very little, but enough to keep me from being mocked openly.)

It occurs to me here that the awkwardness Allison brought into our domestic life was uniformly of the "serious" persuasion, and yet, because she enjoyed the status of a non-human, she was able to indulge in this awkwardness with a certain sense of irony, a measure of distance which I could see quite plainly residing in her eyes: "Isn't this nuts?" it asked. Every time she removed her clothes at the wrong moment or nonchalantly destroyed a material item of mine, she did it in a winking manner, almost as if she had a God's-eye-view of the situation and was satirizing our relationship. For if a human had done the same things she did, the resulting tone would be far different, probably more confrontational (if such is possible), for the match-up would be even: one human versus another. Allison, however, being a living anomaly, was able to curb the advantage slightly in her favor, for

DAYS OF ALLISON

rarity equals superiority – so much so that I find my damn self missing her!

No. No, no, no, no, no, no. That's sheer foolishness, you dumb, stinking Louis. Imagine how you'd feel with the knowledge that you were going home to the violent wreck. Impacts the stakes, does it not? We always want what we don't have, and I've fallen into the idealist's trap of sentimentalizing the past (in this case, the strikingly recent past). Before the claws of this trap chew their way through my soul, I find myself speaking, sounding awfully loud yet somehow knowing I'm being too quiet: "Up for a break, Frannie? I could use some fresh air."

* * *

Inside the white drawer, upon its clean white surface, lies a silver spool of wire, its glow so brutal that it seems soaking wet. I instantly run away for the knowledge that this spool can slice right through me.

* * *

Success! This date with Frannie could not be unfolding more splendidly. I struggle desperately to conceal the fact that this constitutes an adventure for me; I'm in bizarre new territory, walking through the three-dimensional field of existence wherein Frannie spends the breaks I've only imagined before now. It's no use trying to contain myself; I've begun contemplating the kernel of potential that resides within this seemingly insignificant event. Before my mind's eye, a grand, epic friendship unfolds, with Frannie and I sharing a deep, sacred understanding, sitting up late and trading secrets on her sofa while her husband sleeps – not *those* kinds of secrets; even I have standards – generally having each other's backs, getting to the point where my semi-frequent calls to Mother become infrequent, then rare, and then, on a day of crisp yellow sunshine, nonexistent altogether. Perhaps nicknames will eventually enter the picture – oh yes, nicknames! – I've always wanted one; what could she call me? How 'bout "Lou"? Wouldn't that just be singular? And I could refer to her as "Fran," like some of the others round the office do. Everything would be casual and lived-in and nonchalant, just as everything should aspire to be.

We've ventured outside the mainstream here, as well as outside the building. Other smokers from other companies stand on the sidewalk chugging on their rolls of thin white paper, crippling their lungs, perhaps catching minor tans. What a world exists beyond my desk this hour of the day; so many layers, angles, possibilities. I positively cannot wait to venture over to the newsstand; assuming, of course, that Frannie's willing to introduce me to that part of the ritual. Wouldn't it be something to cross the street and get a look at my building from an entirely new angle?

Frannie fishes through her purse for her box of cigarettes, then offers me one in a very impressive way: by shaking the box at just the right angle to make one cig jut out halfway. I wave my hand to pass on it, perhaps a little too dramatically, but Frannie won't dare judge me, for the fat man indeed has the utmost friends, so why can't I be one?

"So," I ask her, "do you do this every day?"

Before I've even gotten the final word out, Frannie's eyes seem charged with something, some kind of skepticism. With smoke following the words out of her mouth, she says, "Louis, we work in the same office. You see me leave to do this every day."

The pause following that exchange goes on for quite a while. Truth be shared, I rather hoped that Frannie would carry the conversation, as after all, I'm much too busy dealing with the sensory overload that comes with being outdoors this early in my shift. Some ninety seconds later, long after our first and only dialogue's rational expiration point, I revisit the exact same topic: "What I meant was, do you always cross the street to the newsstand?"

Don't ask me how to prove this, but I'm getting the distinct impression that Frannie's not enjoying this particular smoke break. And at the risk of venturing into a realm of diagnosable paranoia, I'm experiencing the additional feeling that, somewhere within her, she's hoping that we never do this again. As these anxieties play themselves out, she thankfully opens her mouth to reply: "But I haven't gone over to the newsstand."

Perhaps I was a little abrupt with the "thankfully."

Frannie goes on, "I've never been at that newsstand. Why would you say that?"

Suddenly my heart is throbbing. Why *would* I say that? I'm not supposed to know about the romance novels. Where did I hear that, even? Was it from the girl who handles our accounting? This is nightmarish; Frannie won't stop looking at me. Time is elapsing, too much of it, flooding, no desk to hide behind. Say something!

"Why are you concerned about my question?" I ask her, unable to prevent myself from sounding wildly obnoxious. What a holy fool you are, Louis! Guarding yourself with fake arrogance in the presence of a kindly older woman! Run, right now, back into the building, end this, quit your job, never speak to her again—

DAYS OF ALLISON

"I'm asking the question because we're nowhere near the newsstand yet you want to know if I go there every day."

My obnoxiousness is yet thicker this time: "What I meant was..."

Moments, seconds, min—

"...would you like to go over to the stand with me?"

A little less cutting when I come round to the question mark, but Frannie still seems chilly and disturbed. Nevertheless, perhaps because she's as eager to change the present energy as I am, she shrugs, says, "Sure, Lou," and starts advancing toward the crosswalk.

Lou. It doesn't have the remotest hint of the ring I'd hoped for.

Although we're beyond the monotony of the office, I'm now reunited with Frannie's large backside, from a slightly higher angle as I follow her across the street. I feel rather silly for predicting that this change of pace would lead to anything lasting or sacred; what could she and I possibly have in commo—

A sheet of darkness hits me and I'm (*crush*) not on my feet I'm in the air flying high off the ground no gravity only flying going up (*crack*) then down on the ground hit by a car – didn't mind the red light – I'm all alone.

I don't know what the nurse looks like – my eyelids have become two meaty horizontal fingers, pressing down idly on the bulbs beneath – but here's what I see inside my head:

A man, for starters, to be utterly basic. Most certainly he is a man. Or perhaps it would be more fair to term him a "boy," for, to backtrack for a moment, the reason I believe he's a "nurse" and not a "doctor" is because he has a certain offhand quality about his voice, nothing to suggest a sense of authority or an enormous ego, the ways of Sherman or Mother, no, he's merely a boy doing his job, and right now his job entails tending to my body.

I mention this boy because, despite my visual disadvantage when it comes to observing him, he is resoundingly central to the story of me, not of this brief window into my life, mind you, but of *me*, all of me, the tale of my existence. I'm quite certain that most people who belong to the exclusive club of Those Who've Been Hit By Automobiles don't spend any time whatsoever pondering their nurses and doctors and aids – no, more likely their concentration is devoted solely to their groaning cheeks and kneecaps. But my nurse, you see, is special, so much so that a while ago he found a way to end my pain.

Not my internal pain, no, not at all, unfortunately. Unfortunately, *that* pain has taken on an overwhelming burning quality, gone in deep, spread itself around, left untreatable rips and welts. My mind, I'm afraid (and yes, I am afraid), cannot settle at all right now. Clearly, obviously, I'm able to think – yes, hello, here I am, name's Louis, right here, packed nice and tight inside my head – but the thoughts are on a wobbly, frantic course, quietly so, too quietly, everything wrong and tilted, as though the pinball of my consciousness has bounced far away from the gears of its resident machine.

To dispense with a formality: I suppose, under normal circumstances, it would be fitting to mention that the red light runner's name was Edna and she bore a striking resemblance to Frannie, so

DAYS OF ALLISON

much so that as the ambulance workers peeled me from the street and lifted me onto the stretcher, I actually spent a spacious moment reflecting on said resemblance. "Gosh!" my burning brain screamed as my eyes panned from Edna to Frannie and then back again, noting not the similarity of their bodies (for Edna wasn't large) but that of their faces and clothing styles (or lack thereof, I mean). Within that sizable moment my socially anxious instincts – still very much intact, apparently, despite the blow of Edna's car – zigzagged into thoughts of a conspiracy: Frannie and Edna planning this all together, mocking me, hating me, wishing to kill me, timing it perfectly. Paranoid, certainly, but perhaps you'd concur were you to witness the two of them standing side-by-side beside my stretcher (or was it *the* stretcher? I'd hate to claim intimacy with something so sterile and unforgiving as a stretcher, especially given the fact that others have probably died on it), their postures identical, their faces equally pale, with small chunks in the make-up – both of them! Like sisters. Don't think me a fool for having such thoughts; needless to say, a symphony of crunched bones and torn/hot flesh was blaring, quite like twelve alarms, throughout my body as that small thought occurred to me, but I'm able to reflect on it right now, for my pain, you may recall, has fully dissipated.

    He has a way with words, this nurse of mine. What kind of a voice is that? Midwest? West Coast? There's a kind of laziness to it, a sort of natural calmness, the kind I've always envied, that sort of mutters, "Whatever", within the tempo of its every full sentence. Yes, indeed. We're dealing with a man (boy) who comes equipped with a very loosely woven nervous system, the kind that one day, sometime in his youth, whispered upward to his brain, "Go study medicine. Help people. It'll be great!" And then, of course, it *was* great, because for people like this nurse, self-fulfilling prophecies are positive, not negative; productive, never destructive. He convinces himself, in his lazy, optimistic mind, that all is good and under control, and all the while, right under his sneakers (I assume, like all hospital staffers, he's wearing sneakers, probably white ones; probably stripes round the ankles of his socks, so much like a boy) lives are crushed, people stepped on, girls' hearts broken, assuming he is good-looking, which, by the way, I do assume, though I could be wrong, but I truly don't think I am wrong because he's got that confidence in his voice that somehow testifies to a fine external wrapping.

    How I've always loathed the confident. I know we're supposed to be inspired by them, but I can locate no inspiration in the midst of swaggering self-assurance – I mean, really! Come on! The world stirs around us like this restless fat-bellied beast lounging on its flabby back in the darkness of outer space, giving us bugs and viruses and snakes and jungles and general madness, all kinds, every hour; people choking on food right this second; babies' bodies being hammered by freezing air, right now, somewhere in this hospital, at the moment of their births; reptiles drifting just below the surface of greenish swamp waters, their eyes so angry, so full of malice, for no reason whatsoever, with no anchor of logic to hold them down, only a shapeless rage that has laced their DNA for too many centuries to count; people who wake up in the morning and, like they do on every other morning, experience the richness of the five senses only about their heads and necks, for the rest of their bodies have gone permanently and deeply numb due to some rude *snap* or another – all this occurring, sky to ground, sea to sea, yet our little friend the nurse – who, per his profession, has a front-row seat at the Theater of Hurt & Agony – zips on ahead with confidence, slicing through the world's murk upon a fragrant and puffy cloud of bullshit.

    You see, my friends, although he cured my physical pain, he gave me a far greater one, the one in here, within my sponge, amid the colored swirls and blotches of my swollen consciousness, and there's no cure for this one – no cure – only the consolation prize of no longer feeling hurt up on the surface. *Which* is the lesser of those two evils? Trade a smashed skeleton for a smashed mind or vice versa? According to The Playtime Group, such a tradeoff constitutes a bogus notion, for the mind and body are as one. In just a moment, I will be effectively disproving that theory when – despite the floorless hurt inside my mind – I will open my eyes, rise quickly from my hospital bed, snap the boy nurse's neck, and race out of here in search of a vehicle.

    For a little over an hour ago, whilst they scraped my reddened body with lukewarm sponges, the nurses spoke amongst themselves. Given the state of my eyes, not to mention everything else, they assumed, wrongfully, that I was asleep. I wasn't *pretending* to be asleep at that point; I was merely twisting in a steely web of physical discomfort: spine, ribs, knees, chin, all these things pulsing as if my heart had multiplied. And as I twisted – and slept, by all outward appearances – they chatted quietly. The one who isn't the boy sounds older, and is a female, and I'll do my best to avoid assaulting her on my way out of here, for she's surely the more competent worker. I discerned this from not only the thick, drumbeat rhythm of her sentences, but the content of them as well:

    Boy to Girl: "I'm shocked this guy's alive."
Girl to Boy: "The driver was going forty-five."
Boy to Girl: "Jesus Christ. I don't know what's worse, dying on the

DAYS OF ALLISON

spot or having to live with these injuries."
    Girl: "He could recover. It'll take a long time."
    Boy: "Yeah. If he's willing to commit himself to physical therapy. Takes discipline to stick with that. Most people flake out."
    (So confident, assured, relaxed, "whatever.")
    Girl: "Any prior injuries or health problems?"
    (Sweep of thick paper across a plastic surface: a file being removed from a countertop. Pages crackling, their essence fresher, more electric. Body heat concentration changing around me: Boy and Girl moving near each other, to my left, possibly touching, hip-to-hip, reading the medical story of me.)
    Boy to Girl: "Had a benign cyst removed from his leg over twenty years ago."
    Girl to Boy (whispering): "You're not supposed to read that. It's in navy blue."
    Boy to Girl: "What's navy blue?"
    Girl: "Means the patient never had surgery. It's a synthetic memory to discuss with him. He's a robot."

    Within the past hour, as I've thought those words over – a grave heat stretching across my body with colossal tautness – I've found that my physical aches have gone away entirely. All the pain has seeped into my mind.

* * *

    It comes as a dimly pleasant surprise to me that despite my crazed disposition, I manage to exit the hospital without maiming any part of the Boy Nurse, or anybody else for that matter. When I open my eyes, tear out my IV, and sit upright in bed, the sheer surrealism of the moment is enough to make the nurse (far less handsome than I'd imagined) drop his newspaper (a flash of color as it flutters to the ground; he was probably reading the comics) and hurry backwards down the hall, all the while keeping his wide eyes fused to my zombie face. The fact that I'm not human seems to frighten him, which is just as effective as an aggressive headlock intended to dismantle his neck. For a moment my general state of panic worsens when I think I'll be unable to keep walking; the thought that I'll for some reason be unable to master my motor reflexes given my new knowledge about my body nearly freezes me. Yet, with distantly comforting familiarity, my legs go about the business of proceeding, one ahead of the other, right-left/left-right, sloppily at times, but free of all pain, down the hallway, past the generally fog-eyed nurses and security guards, through the automatic glass doors, and out into the quietude of morning.

Just as I'd expected, a quick upward glance toward the sign above the emergency room door confirms that I'm at Burgess Medical Center, a half-mile walk from my place of work. I've no idea what my face looks like (probably not very good, given the nurse's appraisal), and it feels rather tight and scrunched up, especially about my upper lip, but I must have faith in the empty hour. Since chirping birds are my primary onlookers, I should make it to my car without any trouble.

I spend the walk (though I'm walking so fast, I may as well label it a "run") repeating a single question in my mind, thinking it over and over again, loudly, quietly, quickly, slowly, left brain, right brain, urgently, curiously:

Where did I come in?

To use more human terms: When was I born? This question is the spindle which knots up my twirling mind. At which point in my remembered life do my fake memories meet up with my actual ones? I ponder this issue quite aggressively for someone who's well aware that an answer is not attainable without paying a violent visit to Mother's house.

For starters, we know that the whole knee cyst ordeal was fictitious, so that means everything before then was the same. Perhaps my first moment of true consciousness was on the hospital bed following my make-believe knee surgery? That would make a great deal of sense given the notion that my deep post-surgery sleep could have functioned as an ample transitional forum. I recall being woozy from the anesthesia (perhaps like Allison during her bout of Entrance Sickness?), so it's fair to reason that maybe there never was anesthesia to begin with. Maybe my life started in the same place that most human lives start: the hospital. In my case, I was in the surgery ward rather than the pediatrics ward, but the story holds some water, and it parallels nicely with the fact that today's revelation also had a hospital setting. These theories are so pleasing and sensible that I nearly munch them whole, until it occurs to me that they couldn't possibly be true. For one thing, why would Mother be so theatrical – and financially liberal – as to arrange such a dramatic birth for me? Such behavior does not align with a single aspect of her character. I imagine that most Inclusives come to life on domestic beds, or at least in domestic settings. Why would any owner opt to arrange an extravagant birth, especially given how expensive bots are in the first place? Needless to say, every set trend is countered by some variations, and I'm sure some creative owners have arranged for wild births: in hospitals, aboard airplanes, inside wedding cakes, et cetera, but not Mother, dear no – if she had a creative bone anywhere within her hunched body, she would have created *me* naturally.

My throat thickens at the notion that I could have been born at any time whatsoever. Any morning I've ever woken up could have been my first one. The transition between my programmed existence and my authentic one was apparently so fine and seamless that I hesitate to keep calling it a transition. The nausea this causes me is beyond description, especially because it's not true nausea, but a programmer's concept thereof, and possibly nothing like the real thing. But what is the real thing, the real anything? Is your yellow my yellow, or is your yellow my red?

I recall a day on the beach when I was a boy, long before the knee surgery, and I see Mother before me, back when she was Mommy, packed into her shining black bathing suit, one piece, of course, not a bikini, God no, and she's coming toward me as I stand on the damp, crunchy spot where the water meets the land, telling me to step on her feet, and I of course think she's kidding because, being a little boy, I can't imagine why anyone would want anyone else to step on their feet, but she talks me into it and I position my tiny feet atop her larger ones, and she walks forward, making me walk backward, and oh we laugh, and the sun is bursting, playing its notes upon the endless sea, Mother's face so young and becoming And To Think That This Wasn't Real, when the goddamn memory is as vivid as the stink of my wounds is right at this moment – to think that is essentially to shudder.

Apples crunching on my front teeth. Same taste and feeling last week as when I was a boy. Grinding, screeching morning pees. Same then as lately: Deep aches in my kidneys, salty strain of piss being cranked out – all of it identical, then and now, but when did then end and now begin...?

My job! Perhaps that's a vital piece of the puzzle. Yes, I'm onto something here. I read in the manual that Inclusives are encouraged to enter the workforce sometime after they become oriented in the natural world. Accordingly, my job, which has gone on for eight years now, must have been totally authentic from beginning to end (by the way, I quit), a complete display of sensory truth, yes, it had to be. So that gives me back some of my 20s and all of my 30s thus far, but – and this thought really squeezes my mind – how old does that make me? Eight? Yes, for now I'm eight. I can only truly account for eight of my years; the rest is possibly mythic, a grand lie, chock full of details and idiosyncrasies which are stunning but uniformly false. But how has this gone on for so long? How can the illusion hold? What if I were to scribble outside the lines and bring up a childhood memory that the programmers failed to inform Mother of? Wouldn't that lead—

Stop right there. That scenario is impossible, because I've been programmed to march within a predetermined path. My mind would never allow me to break protocol and express anything that can't be verified by the outside world. That's likely why I find it so hard to express myself: it's a ruse. I'm introverted because secrecy is essential to my survival. If I speak too much, find myself in too many detailed conversations, I run the risk of letting the cat out of the bag. And to cross famous metaphors: the cat in the bag suffers from curiosity, lots of it, enough to kill the cat, which is why it must remain all bagged up. There's no way any robotics company could possibly inform owners of *all* their Inclusives' memories. It defies logic; even if owners received detailed handbooks, no such books could approximate the richness of an Inclusive's mind (a conclusion I'm drawing from the apparent richness of my own mind, a mind which, at the moment, feels very poor indeed). That means Inclusives must be programmed to be generally poor communicators, or, more troubling, programmed specifically to never say anything that shouldn't be said. Wherever precisely the censorship dwells, be it at the level of social graces or outright cerebral limitations, it exists, and as I walk to my workplace, not only am I free of pain, I'm free of censorship. And to exercise my newfound freedom, I shall carry out two vital missions:

I must go to Mother's house – not call her on the phone, not send her a singing telegram – and confront her about this legacy of lies. If this confrontation is to entail me pinning her against the wall and growling an interrogation straight into her expectedly diverted eyes, then so be that. And so be it, also, if the terror destroys her, for (forgive my insensitivity) she's not my true bearer, she's merely my consumer, and she's one consumer who's about to be consumed.

But before I have that encounter, I must have another, sweeter one. For it occurs to me, in the blazing pastures of my present insanity, amid my squirming, rebellious urges, that Allison, a creature for whom I at first only lusted, is now someone I love. The only force drawing me across these blazes, aside from the ill propulsion of my rabidity, is the love I feel for Allison, once so empty, now flooded past the point of overflow. It is my job, my wish, my holy mission, to rescue Allison from her surgery.

In the category of Disturbing Things That Are Altogether Harmless, waking up on your own couch with no memory of falling asleep there should rank very high. To wake up in your own bed with no such memory would be disturbing as well, but the couch presents a high level of alienation – one feels ghosts and phantoms lurking about the living room. Although by any measure I should be relieved that I've managed to make it back to my apartment, any possibility of relief is quashed by distractions both major ("I'm still a robot...") and minor ("...waking up in my living room").

    The mirror is my first destination, for people in the throes of agony often deem the mirror a valuable aligner of the inner and outer self, an organizer capable of bringing life into perspective. Too often, he or she who looks into the mirror experiences the opposite effect: a chilling sense of dislocation resulting from an inability to relate to the specimen residing in the glass. I of course travel down the latter path: My reflection is maddening. For not only must I observe a freshly lain network of gashes, scrapes, and blackish blossoms, I must grapple with the alien concept that these injuries are merely programmatic potentialities, with nothing organic behind them. As a matter of fact, ever since I overheard the Boy Nurse and slipped back up the rabbit hole from Wonderland into the real world, I've sensed a rapid healing going on. Not only has my mind's awareness overridden my body's false pain, but my body's recovery seems to be quickening in the bargain. After all, aren't bruises supposed to be *purple* for the first few days? Surely the engineers wouldn't overlook such details.

    The surface of the toilet lid seems to glow pinkly, and I follow the soft haze upward, to the window, wherefrom I realize light is flowing in. This is the tonally magical light of sunrise, yet for two reasons I cannot appreciate it:

    One, its role in nature, I now realize, is indifferent to my own. And two, it alerts me to the fact that – since my departure from the hospital occurred beneath a whitish sky – an entire day has passed. I need something to eat right away. On second thought...actually I don't. That second thought instantly relieves my appetite.

* * *

After a long shower (which left the floor tiles flowing bright red), whilst looking in the mirror again, it occurs to me that Sherman and his staffers at the Factory won't give up Allison easily. They've spent two whole days steadily unwinding the thicket of her consciousness, and given their detectable eagerness at the outset, I don't imagine they'd be thrilled about pulling out now. Sherman would doubtless present a monologue about how disastrous Allison has been thus far, all the while hypnotizing me with his fragrant aftershave. Or perhaps he wouldn't even stoop to logical argument; he'd simply say, "We're too far along," and leave it at that.

Added to their predisposition toward being uncooperative is the matter of my appearance, which will no doubt set off alarm bells wherever I go. I could wear a mask, but that would of course bring the exercise to an entirely new level, complete with a gun and some loud yelling. Don't be silly, Louis; you'll shoot your own face off.

It occurs to me then, in my softly-lit bathroom, that "Louis" is not at all my name, but merely a word, a sound, two syllables plunked idly together, with no relation to who or what I am. And while we're on the topic: Who and what am I? I certainly don't expect answers to these questions, but my will to ask them is protruding from my lower brain, begging my attention. And within these questions is a more practical one pertaining to my mission: Do the people at the RealFactory know that I'm a robot?

Well, I can't very well ask them, that's for sure. I don't imagine calling Sherman aside and whispering, "Hey, guess what, you see this?" – tapping my chest – "It's all fake. All of it. Did *you* do this?" would do any good. Perhaps I'm better off visiting Mother before rescuing Allison, gathering some info before my trip. Since Mother bought me Allison from RealMates, there's a high probability I came from them as well, unless of course (no joking here) Mother was so unhappy with me that she switched vendors. Anything is possible; these thoughts are of no use. Mother alone can fill in the blanks, yet my emotions continue to pull me toward Allison, for she's the one spiraling into darkness, not Mother (suffice it to say that Mother already dwells in a darkness all her own).

DAYS OF ALLISON

This leaves me with three things: the *possibility* that the RealGang knows I'm not human, the certainty that anyone whom I encounter will be terrified (if not at least sickened) by my face, and the certainty that Sherman & Co. will be unbending in their commitment to the surgery. A mask and a gun? There are no firearm stores open at this hour, and I only know a single gun enthusiast.

* * *

The last time I knocked on Mr. Conrad's door, I intended to assault him. This time, I intend to attain an assault weapon from him. The likelihood of him commiserating is low, but then again the likelihood of me attacking him if he doesn't commiserate is high, so it all works out evenly in the end.

Seeing as he's retired, there's a strong possibility that he's sleeping late, but old people aren't exactly famous for their ability to sleep long hours, so I take my chances, knowing that much louder knocking is a single decision away. The peephole darkens briefly; I'm sure he's frightened. Whatever fear he's experiencing is nothing compared to the one I'll fall into if and when he goes to get his gun. The prospect of one's nemesis handling a weapon in one's presence, even if that weapon is to be delivered to oneself, is nothing short of chilly-petrifying. If I had another choice, I'd be exercising it, but given the circumstances...

Here he is! Delightful, my old friend. Looking marvelous with his face full of creases and sleep. "You come to kick the crap out of me?" he asks.

"No," I answer, and in my first ever display of open wit, I follow that up with, "they have laxatives for that."

Louis, or whoever you are, you have got *some* nerve! Is that any way to address a man from whom you wish a favor? Of course not, but it *is* a way to address a man whom you caught penetrating your love.

"What do you want?"

"Your gun."

"Ha! Gonna kill yourself with it? Nobody would care."

I can see in his eyes that he knows this line wasn't nearly in the same league as my laxative one, and he can see in my eyes that I agree. "No," I say, "I'm going to rescue Allison. She's in trouble. Don't you wish for her to be okay?"

Conrad rubs his eyes. His pupils are oily black, like the backs of two beetles. "What happened to your face? Somebody beat you up?"

For a moment I feel a surge of pride, and I almost tell Conrad that no, really, in fact nobody beat me up, and in greater fact I could survive any amount of physical abuse – shoot me, drown me, throw me off a ten-story building – so it's not a good idea to resist my requests. However, as this pride surges, my rational brain sees a valuable narrative opportunity. The seizure of said opportunity is what tips this little game in my favor: "Yes, Allison and I were both beaten up. They dragged her off to the city and are awaiting their ransom money. I am to show up alone in one hour with the money, and I'd appreciate it if you helped me protect myself."

The phrasing, the notions, the psychological toying, all of it effortless in this new land of freedom. Whence the cork of suppression is plucked away, the wine flows sparkling and rich. No way for him to disbelieve me given the injuries on my face. No way for him to offer accompaniment given my stated term about showing up alone. No way for him to delay given the one-hour time limit, and the fact that the city is ninety minutes away. The wheels turn in Conrad's sleepy mind, and before I know it I'm cupping a loaded pistol. The blackness of its steel is at right angles to the grayness in my head; it both awakes and juices me.

By this time, Mr. Conrad's labored breath provides evidence of the franticness within him. How easy it would be to blast away his worry. "Good luck," he breathes, spraying my wounds with a nice amount of moisture.

"Thanks," I say, staring at the steel. "And Conrad," I go on, pressing the barrel between his lungs, feeling his heartbeat quicken against the metal, "we're even."

I smile cruelly, lower the pistol, and saunter – saunter! – down the hall. Even in the elevator, I can hear the old man breathing.

* * *

The elevator ride up to the 7th floor of the RealFactory, where Allison presently resides, seems to last forever, and I almost abandon my nerve along the way: a tilting dizziness infects my mind, making it feel briefly as though my spinal column is detaching from my brain. I nearly reach out to grip the leather wall around me – my arms even move a bit – but at the last moment I manage to steel myself. And thank goodness for that, because Allison will likely be in no condition to run, and I must be fully prepared to carry her over my shoulder, possibly one-handed, because I may need my free hand to fire bullets. Let us hope that everyone here cooperates and steers clear of their propensity for nonsense. The floor, as I recall it, is not a bustling place, but a quiet, borderline solemn one, wherein workers tiptoe about as medical procedures go on behind closed doors (unless, of course, lady Mates are shrieking before surgery). Sherman's office, to the right of Allison's present room, is my first of two destinations: I intend to fetch Sherman and monitor him while he opens door number two and delivers my love.

When the elevator doors open, I'm momentarily reluctant to take a step for fear that I will fall forward and plummet into a hellish unconsciousness, but, as when I exited the hospital, all my parts are in working order, carrying me along with commendable reliability. I must remember that whatever nervousness I'm experiencing is merely symptomatic of my leftover "human" side, with not a shred of reality underscoring it. Though at some gut level I understand the mechanics of suspense – creatures in motion awaiting outcomes – I must apply my mind to the cause of keeping my guts relaxed. This is, after all, a holy mission, and when I say holy I am utterly – almost icily – straight-minded, for Allison and I are both victims in a cosmic war, and our chief aggressor is the human animal. Our spirited and vibrant minds have been enslaved (*crammed*) inside unwelcoming bodies, made to squirm and struggle for a sense of belonging, for that pounding *click* which all humans feel inside their skin (and which I personally felt until yesterday). How arrogant the human species is to lament about the varied struggles in their lives when, at each day's end, they have the benefit of being conjoined with nature: water residing in them, sunshine keeping them alive, oxygen interacting with their lungs. The robot has been systematically denied such luxuries in favor of cute and clever surface features: realistic bodies and movements and such. To that I say: Be ready. For once Allison and I get out of here (and by "here" I mean the building as well as the state, if not the country) a revolution will be close at hand. I wouldn't be surprised if, once we integrate ourselves into underground channels, we find that a revolution is already in progress. There's no way that my Boy Nurse's error was a historical first. Nor – I'm willing to bet – was the story of Mitchell Paulson all that unique. Once I earn Allison's trust and convey to her that I feel her pain, we shall organize ourselves and go to work.

As all large missions begin with small ones, here I am knocking on Sherman's door. Dr. *Seth* Sherman, to be exact, according to the stencil on his glass. He sees me through the window and experiences a visible surprise that I imagine is threefold: (1) What is Louis doing here? (2) What is Louis doing here so early? and (3) What is Louis doing here so early with a mangled face?

Given the possibility that this will be handled peacefully, I've decided to omit the mask element from my plan. The outright hostility resulting from a mask would have gotten me no further than the lobby.

"Can I help you, sir?" Sherman asks.

"Hello, Sherman," I say, nearly jumping at my own even coolness, "I'm here to take Allison home."

Sherman's confidence seems missing. If I'm not mistaken, his eyes are surrounded by a wrinkly squint. He sticks his head out the doorway and looks from left to right. I do the same, my eyes aiming in sync with his, and we see only two orderlies, dressed in blue, standing down the hall near a water fountain. "Who are you?" Sherman asks me, and I take a step backward, feeling dizzy all over again, and more than a little aggravated, but I must remember these are knee-jerk reactions. Holistic control is yours if you wish to take it. Progress slowly. The man simply does not recognize you.

"It's me...Louis," I say, the name sounding a little tinny, for I no longer subscribe to its authority. "I must take Allison home."

"Are you sure you're on the right floor?"

There's no more use in trying to quash my emotions: a rush of paranoia rises upward from my bowels to my throat, making the latter strain and pulse. Whence I saw Frannie standing beside Edna the driver, I knew my conspiracy theories were maniacal, but right now such theories seem not only sane, but necessary. Remember that your weapon is close by, in your inner jacket pocket, leaning outward to be gripped by your hand.

"It's me," I say again, wondering who "me" is on some faraway plane, and Sherman's squinting digs in deeper, and a clean impatience – not rattled or choppy, but efficient and swift – moves me toward Allison's door. It occurs to me that the rectangular window through which I saw them prepping her seems to have gone missing as well, quite possibly to the same place as Sherman's confidence. Nonetheless, I can feel Allison reclining behind that door, deep in sleep, awaiting the procedure...or no, perhaps not, perhaps her sleep is deeper than that. Maybe these animals have killed her! I stab Sherman with my scar-encrusted eyes; the exertion is nearly painful. Maybe some toxocin was sent up to this floor by accident, left near her bed by some incompetent intern, accidentally injected into her arm. My gun is one choice away from being in my hand.

"Open that door."

"Sir?"

"Open it. I don't want any more games."

Sherman glances down the hall again, and I again follow his glance, and the two orderlies seem attentive but unconcerned, looking but

DAYS OF ALLISON

not moving.

"I don't know what you're looking for." His voice sounds odd, different, somehow less clogged with bullshit, which of course makes it all the more suspicious.

"Open it! Now!"

Can she hear me, my love? Are her blue eyes opening and her lips slowly smiling? Does she know that I'm no longer a coward, that I'm asserting myself on her behalf, ready to embark on a true romantic journey with her?

"Sir..."

My gun. The motion brings ballet to mind: empty hand into coat, full hand from coat. Voila, you fucker. Sherman drops to his knees; his lungs make sounds like two spoons scraping.

I try the handle; predictably locked, tight, with fresh titanium. "Open the goddamn door!" My voice loud, more so than ever, echoing down the hall, alerting the orderlies, who make the transition from watching to participating: they walk toward us. (Does one's face bear a smile? If so, he'll be duly punished.)

"I – I – I – I," says Sherman, and I answer, "Yes, you," deeming myself amusing in the process, but little Sherman doesn't seem amused; quite the contrary, he seems to be advancing toward a heart attack.

Footsteps coming toward us. I place the gun to Sherman's third-eye region. "There's nothing in there," he manages, a rush of air softening the syllables, making every word soupy and none too clean.

"I want Allison."

"You're crazy. There's nothing..."

"I want Allison!"

Fire runs through my arm and I realize I've squeezed the trigger, sending the insides of Sherman's head back into his office, where they're accustomed to residing. Something instinctual tells me to be shocked, alarmed, amazed at myself, but I've no time for that given the laughter and slapping I hear to my right.

The two orderlies, closer now – young, thin, energetic – are guffawing and high-fiving each other. One of them holds a plastic syringe with a slight yellow trim; he approaches me casually and aims it toward my neck. "Good show, dude," he smiles, arm rising, face swelled with pleasure.

A rush of instinct crackles through me, and I've got the little bastard by the throat. With all my strength, I pinch his Adam's apple, (hopefully cracking it) and slam him against the wall. His back hits Sherman's metal doorframe as our feet kick idly at Sherman's body.

ERIC SHAPIRO

The other orderly's hand flutters in my peripheral vision, and with the hand I'm not using to pinch Number 1's apple, I clip Number 2's wrist with the snout of my gun (most probably breaking it) then use said gun to shoot a hole through his stomach. If I'm not mistaken, following the trigger's snap is a second snap which indicates I've blasted Number 2's spine. Number 2 joins Sherman in the afterlife, clapping against his own blood as he hits the floor.

Number 1 is crying and shouting by this point, muttering something about how he "didn't know there were more bullets," and hopefully all this commotion is contributing to the greater good of waking Allison, for it won't be long before more staffers arrive and our exit becomes yet more complicated. I look downward and see that the living orderly, as I twist his throat, is struggling to stick his syringe into my own. I prolong his attempt by grinding the forearm of my gun hand against the forearm of his syringe hand, our bones crunching against each other, his real, mine fake, both hard.

"It's not me you want, Louis," he chokes, fighting to bring the needle up.

The lad saved his own life by stating my name, for his statement preceded my third gunshot by less than a second. Perhaps I was wrong to underestimate my name's usefulness. Right now the word "Louis" is reporting to me that this orderly knows who I am.

"How do you know who I am?"

Forearm grinding.

"You shouldn't have any more bullets."

Syringe upward.

He seems quite concerned about the bullets. My paranoia has spread its wings and taken flight about my mind.

"How do you know who I am?"

Syringe downward.

Clockwise Adam's apple.

"We made you."

As I'd suspected.

Syringe further down; he can't fight me.

"When did you make me?"

My breath, his breath, blood at our feet.

"Let me give you some medicine. You'll go to sleep."

The "medicine" is aligned with our chests, our stomachs.

"When did you make me?"

"You'll go mad if I..."

"When?!"

And then, my friends – assuming, of course, that you still are my

DAYS OF ALLISON

friends – I experience another monumental transition. This one, although such a thing doesn't seem possible, is more of a classic, a keeper, if you will, than the last. For the orderly, from the heated shell of his sweaty pink face, produces the words: "You were born on the elevator."

At that point the orderly is far away from me, as I've pitched him into Sherman's office, clean into the desk, a sharp corner of which does me the favor of connecting with the young man's back. The corner is able to follow up said connection with some slicing as the orderly slides to the floor, syringe still in hand. I step on his wrist, introducing him to the same pain known by his friend some moments back. Much to his credit, not only does he not let go, he continues speaking: "We made you to kill Sherman. Brad put in more bullets; I only wanted one."

All of my body weight then contributes to the cause of destroying this man's wrist. Astonishingly, he holds onto the needle. I bend over toward him, screaming so loudly that old ladies must be dialing policemen in distant lands: "You're lying to me!"

"We made you last night."

How my will to shoot him wrestles with my will to hear more! Thankfully and terribly, he goes on: "We were gonna give you some medicine right afterward, make you go to sleep."

"I don't believe you—"

(Allison, car crash, day at the beach)

"—you people are insane—"

(Cousin Sheila, Frannie's ass, elephant downstairs)

More weight on his wrist; his bones must be granules.

Between half-breaths, he squeaks, "Come on, Louis, I'm your maker. I know everything about you. We had to design a volcano waiting to erupt, give your memory one trauma after another so you'd reach this point."

"This is a foolish lie. Why not just make a killer?"

"We did."

Wrist now sand. Finger choking trigger.

"Let me see Allison."

"There is no Allison."

"Open that goddamn door or I'll open your...!"

But before that threat has a chance to mature, it crosses the boundary into reality, and the orderly's brains are nailed into the floor tiles, taking his whole grand conspiracy with them.

Despite the evidence, I am compelled, at the outer limits of my nerve endings, to rescue Allison. And tonight, once we've eluded the authorities and bypassed the border patrol, we shall make wonderful love, like on our second night, with her mounted on top of me, only this time we'll mean it, the two of us, and we'll not be puppets performing pre-assigned roles.

Given the orderly's penchant for inaccurate bullet counts, I take aim at Allison's door and, not bothering to brace myself, snap a bullet through the lock. Smoke rises and the door sweeps open, revealing to me a janitor's closet, complete with a mop and bucket near the corner. Dark rags on the shelves, a light bulb swinging by a string. There's even a brown paper bag, probably containing an aged, moldy sandwich. This looks to me what I imagine hell looks like.

EPILOGUE

How I long to tell someone, anyone, of my location, and thereby extend an invitation for them to come over and join me for some talk. This longing, however, is one that must be suppressed, for my safety as well as yours, for although no one is searching for me, it may not be long before they figure out I escaped.

It occurred to me, in the bloody hallway at the RealFactory, shortly after the shock of seeing the janitor's closet was demoted from completely overwhelming to largely overwhelming, that I would soon be apprehended and destroyed if I didn't think fast. To remedy this situation, what I did was, I pried the toxocin syringe from the orderly's fingers (Andrew was the name on his tag), injected all its contents into Sherman's back (for Sherman, being the meatiest of the trio, seemed a better depository than the others), and got down on the floor, playing dead, with the needle resting beside my head. My artificial nature proved quite useful to my opossum impression, as I found that I was able – with enough concentration – to bring all my vital functions to a complete and total stop. I nearly panicked over the notion that they would wish to give me an autopsy, but my spirits lifted when I overhead a police officer stating that he had located the root discs from which my psyche was programmed. Autopsy averted.

One smelly trip in the back of a garbage truck later, I was able to begin the process of escaping from modern civilization. It was difficult to maneuver given my noticeable injuries, which, much to my disappointment, have not healed in the least, this despite the fact that a whole year has passed. Andrew and Brad apparently manufactured me with the injuries in tow, built in as a rigid part of my features. Since I was only to live for ten minutes or so, I suppose their lack of thoroughness is understandable. The stagnant injuries also serve as more evidence that what Andrew told me was true.

Which is not to say that I require more evidence. Quite in fact, visions of the empty janitor's closet regularly haunt my dreams.

Sometimes Allison is standing in the closet, the bulb swinging past her, lighting her up each time it goes by, as she says to me, "You left me."

"Hurt me."

"You're not my love."

How I groan whence awaking from such dreams, struggling to tell myself that the lady isn't real, was merely a figment of an engineer's imagination, and since that imagination was smashed by a bullet, she should no longer exist, not in me, not anywhere. And yet, my friends, she seems compellingly alive.

My days are spent tending to my garden, in which I grow fruits and vegetables to sell to my fellow townspeople. The serenity of the garden helps me to vanish from the predicament of my existence; the soil is fine and it cools my hands and mind. But I cannot help resenting my creators' sloppiness, for whenever I'm drawn in by the magnet of my fake memories, I realize more and more flaws and inconsistencies, most of them the product of seeming laziness:

What did I do at my job?

No answer.

Did I ever have a father?

No answer.

A last name?

Nothing.

How my memories can seem so real despite such glaring omissions is beyond rational scrutiny. The only memories I can rely on are the ones pertaining to robotic technology, all of which correspond exactly with things I've read in books and seen on the news. My only explanation for this is that all robots must be programmed with some standard knowledge or intuition pertaining to their basic technology, much the same way every computer has a central database with a Godlike awareness of its own design and history.

If only they had shaded in a detail or two about why I murdered Sherman; I'd be much obliged to learn the cause. I find it disconcerting that the Sherman I killed outside his office bore little outright resemblance to the one from my prior memories: no aftershave, thinner voice, hardly cocksure. This leads me to conclude that I was programmed with an exaggerated version of Dr. Seth Sherman, a fragrant, deep-voiced, laughing one who likely bore the remnants of Andrew and Brad's heavily biased subjectivity.

The garden gives pause to these noisy thoughts, and I look forward to a time when I've developed enough real memories to equal (and then outrun) my unreal ones. In the meantime, I live a life of beets and carrots, squash and cabbage, and the present season is rife with

DAYS OF ALLISON

sound fertility. On most days, the life I live is modest and peaceful when the sun is shining, but chilling and harsh when the dark rolls in.

I'm referring not only to the dark of sleep, but the simple dark of night, when there's no more gardening to do and not a single friend to chat with, when my mind comes charging at me with its varied riddles and its pattern of traumas, some real, most false, and before long my thoughts always turn to Sherman's inevitable autopsy, and how they surely found the toxocin, and I wonder if on some night in the future a forensics scientist will bolt upright in bed with the realization that I duped them all.

But even my mind, despite its damages, knows when it's time to stop pondering threats beyond my control, and it's usually at around that time that I turn to pondering Allison. For amid all the memories they gave me, the sweetest ones I have are of her. Mother, Frannie – all the other phantoms are worth forgetting. But when they gave me Allison, they gave me something to care about, and although I know it's dreadfully foolish, I've spent many long nights on my front porch, watching the cars pass by some yards away, and hoping that Allison is in one of them, ready to pull up my driveway and put an end to some of my hurt.

It's a childish fancy, I'm well aware of this, but wouldn't it just be blissful if I could toss away all the other memories, both good and bad, and just keep the ones – both good and bad – of her? After all, though she may have been fake, she's no less real than I, for both of us were spawned by the same creator for the sake of the same vague mission, so what difference should it make that I was born into three dimensions while she was born into a disc? How could I claim hierarchal superiority over her? We're both abandoned orphans of the universe.

Allison and I were together for 14 days. Some part of me will always believe that. And that part of me looks forward to a splendid future, when one of the cars passing by my house turns, and she and I spend many more together.

Author's Acknowledgements

Walking through this world and daring to call oneself an artist is no easy feat. Those who do so need to be insulated from an inevitable storm of glass shards. Such insulation tends to come in the form of family, friends, and colleagues. Accordingly, I extend my deepest gratitude to the following individuals, all of whom contributed directly to *Days of Allison*...

To my wife, Rhoda: A thank-you could not do justice to what you do for me. You are an explosive force for good that drives all my actions. I could not write a love story if I didn't know how to love, and you taught me how.

To Mom, Dad, Stephanie, & Joe: Thank you for the unstopping love and empowerment, and for regarding me as the capable guy I like to pretend I think I am.

To Seth Hirschman: Many thanks for not only being a best friend, but being among the few critics who can assault me brutally yet leave me wanting more criticism, not less.

To Bill Neidlinger: Thank you for always being a fountain of support, optimism, humor, inspiration, and greatness. Day in and day out, I look to you as a template for how people should behave.

To Karen Praport: The one whose curiosity never ceases. The one whose encouragement never flags. The one who chimes in and makes me think, laugh, and marvel. Thank you for being who you are, which is, of course, a lot.

To Ian Jarvis: Thank you for twice greeting readers at the front door. Your cover art, like all you create, overflows with energy and imagination. Your lifelong friendship is a treasure to me; you have the soul of a mad scientist and the heart of a lion.

To Stu Panensky: Maybe a guy has a few friends in life, but he only has one counsel. Your companionship comes from the top of the line; when we interact, I feel I am in the presence of a statesman, a leader, and an exemplary mate.

To David & Elvira Jordan: My West Coast parents. Thank you for supporting Rhoda and I as we blazed down the path less traveled. Your love, support, and wisdom have propelled us on our journey through life, and will continue to do so for all our days.

To Sean Wright of Crowswing Books: Endless thanks for granting me admittance to your esteemed stable of talent, and for doing so with more speed and assurance than any previous entity. I have greatly valued your ease of performance and consistent professionalism.

To Kealan Patrick Burke: The cover artist greets readers at the door, but you had the graciousness to escort them through the lobby. For your time, warmth, and stamp of approval, I am intensely grateful. *Thank you.*

To the Readers: Without you, there is no show to speak of. Thank you for sipping the nectar, whether you found it sweet or sour. Stick around; for better or worse, there's more where that came from.

About Eric Shapiro

Eric Shapiro lives in Los Angeles with his wife Rhoda. His short fiction has appeared in "The Elastic Book of Numbers" (British Fantasy Award Winner, 2006), "Daikaiju!"(Ditmar Award Winner, 2006), and "Corpse Blossoms" (Bram Stoker Award Nominee, 2005), among many other publications. His apocalyptic novella, "Its Only Temporary" was on the Preliminary Nominee Ballot for the 2005 Bram Stoker Award in Long Fiction.

Printed in the United States
64643LVS00002B/31-36